She momentarily wondered how Jan could have willingly given this up. One moment she fought to breathe, the next found her caught up in the ardor, no longer reluctant or shy. Shrugging out of her shorts and T-shirt when Shelley did, she pressed against her — skin on skin. Warm and sweaty and comforting. She became lost in the kissing, willingly stalled, and Shelley had to lead her to the next stage. After they climaxed, she lay speechless at their having made love at all and would have gladly started over.

Unbidden, the shyness returned. Their relationship had been altered. No longer were they just friends. When Shelley rolled away from her onto her back, she took the gesture as dismissal.

By Reservation Only

Jackie
Calhoun

THE NAIAD PRESS, INC.
1998

Printed in the United States of America on acid-free paper
First Edition

Editor: Lila Empson
Cover designer: Bonnie Liss (Phoenix Graphics)
Typesetter: Sandi Stancil

Library of Congress Cataloging-in-Publication Data

Calhoun, Jackie.
    By reservation only / by Jackie Calhoun.
        p.   cm.
    ISBN 1-56280-191-0 (pbk.)
    1. Lesbians—Wisconsin—Fiction. I. Title.
PS3553.A3985B9   1997
813'.54—dc21   97-40426
                                                                                    CIP

For Diane,
who named this book

About the Author

Jackie Calhoun is the author of *Lifestyles, Second Chance, Sticks and Stones, Friends and Lovers, Triple Exposure, Changes, Love or Money* and *Seasons of the Heart*. She has stories in five Naiad anthologies. Calhoun lives in Wisconsin with her partner.

Books by Jackie Calhoun

Lifestyles
Second Chance
Sticks and Stones
Friends and Lovers
Triple Exposure
Changes
Love or Money
Seasons of the Heart

This is a work of fiction.

Part I

I

A cool wind belied the date — May fourth. Wrapping her arms around herself, Shelley studied the small lake before her. It glistened, then darkened, as clouds scudded across the sun. The trees on the other side rippled in reflection. A few reeds poked out of the shallows. The sandy beachfront at her feet was held in place by tall red pines, their knobby roots evidence of erosion. Leaning over, she swished a hand in the icy water.

She'd driven from Milwaukee to look at this property left to her by an uncle she'd met only

3

occasionally on holidays and then at her parents' funeral. She thought she knew why he had chosen her as his heir instead of her two brothers. He'd been her mother's brother, sometimes the butt of her father's jokes. Her mother's face would darken with anger, and her father would belatedly apologize. She hadn't understood then. She did now. If there is a gay gene, she'd inherited it through her mother's family tree.

Reinforcing her belief in such a hereditary factor was her only child, Joe, who represented the third generation of family homosexuality as she knew it. It should have brought them closer, should have made him more forgiving, but it hadn't. She still woke in the night, regretting her choices and their consequences. At forty, after years of denial, she'd left Joe's father for the first available lesbian. She'd met Jan Crabbe later.

The resort, called Pine Shores, lay on the north side of Arrowhead Lake. The beach faced the sun, but the small weathered cottages that surrounded her uncle's log house were nestled among towering pines. A bed of needles softened the ground.

Plunking down on a metal chair that had survived the spring thaw, she considered what to do. She had decisions to make. Should she sell the place? Should she keep it and let someone else run it? Should she attempt to make a go of it herself?

Jan had made it clear that she wouldn't leave the city. If Shelley took over the resort, she'd do it without Jan, with whom she'd lived for five years. She was too entrenched in her job, too enmeshed in the politics of lesbianism and feminism. Jan had lived in Milwaukee all her life. Their friends were there.

4

She loved the multicultural offerings, the large and diverse population, the ethnic foods, even the noise.

Paralyzed by indecision, Shelley grew colder in the fading day. Already this place, an unexpected gift, was becoming an albatross about her neck. As the sun slid behind a bank of clouds, she started toward the house where she planned to stay the night. Earlier she'd walked through it, turning up the heat, stashing food in the fridge for a brief stay. Now she stepped into the warmth, switching on lights as she passed through the living room into the kitchen.

The inside walls were pine, the floors hardwood except for the linoleum in the kitchen and bath. The front porch cut off the sunlight that otherwise might have reached the living room. But the view of the lake from the windows made up for the darkness of the interior. Tomorrow she would investigate the rental cabins.

As day turned into night, she warmed her first meal in the microwave. The phone rang when she sat down to eat.

"May I speak to Scott, please?"

She swallowed a mouthful of Gourmet Delight and tasted remorse at being the bearer of bad news. "Scott died a month ago. I'm his niece, Shelley."

She thought she detected a slight moan in the pause that followed. "I'm shocked. And sorry. My name's Bill Hailey. I have a reservation for two weeks in July, and Ted and I wanted to come Memorial Day weekend. Scott always opened up for us."

"Did he?" She had a lot to learn if she was going to be in charge.

"What happened?" Bill asked.

"To my uncle? He had a massive heart attack while carrying in wood." She had a sneaking suspicion from this man's voice that he too was gay.

"Who's going to run the place now?"

"I haven't decided yet."

"Well, you're one lucky lady to be able to decide. Can we come for Memorial Day? We always take number eight, the cabin on the west end."

"Give me your name again and phone number. I'll let you know."

She finished eating, changed the sheets on her uncle's bed, watched a little TV, read a chapter in her library book, and fell asleep.

Waking to the clamor of birdsong, she thought she would tell Jan that the outdoors could be as noisy as the city. Nature isn't silent. Wind soughed in the pines, blue jays screeched, squirrels chirred, and crows cawed from somewhere off in the woods. Yesterday she'd lifted her head as several sandhill cranes flew over and made peculiar clacking sounds. Maybe if she pointed the sounds out she could sway Jan to see things her way. Isn't it every person's dream to own her own business? Here she'd been presented with an incredible opportunity with no cost involved, other than paying taxes out of her uncle's estate.

She walked from one cottage to another, finding each cold and musty and an exact replica of the one before. All had two small bedrooms with a bath between, a kitchen, a living/dining area, and a screened-in front porch. Each cottage contained appliances, an electric wall-heater, dishes, utensils, and pots and pans.

Eight aluminum boats were overturned on the

beach. She looked in a storage building and saw small motors for each boat, oars stacked in one corner with anchors nearby, and life jackets hanging from hooks on the walls. What a deal. She'd have to find out what her uncle charged to rent one of these cabins.

Also stored here on a trailer was a boat with high seats, a fifty horsepower motor, and an electric trolling motor. In a far corner was a Ski-Doo snowmobile. She assumed the boat and snowmobile had been her uncle's and were now hers. Walking around the boat slowly, she admired this new find. She was discovering unexpected riches. She had no use for the noise and stench of snowmobiles, but she examined this one with interest. It might be a necessity in the winter.

Returning to the house, she searched her uncle's file cabinet and desk, coming up with registration books for the past ten years. Sitting in his office chair, she paged through this year's bookings. There were names, addresses, and phone numbers. All had paid one hundred dollars in advance. The summer was pretty well filled. She wondered if she should send these people notification that Scott Smith was deceased and that she, Shelley Carpenter-Benson, was now running the resort. She would ask for their expectations and try to fulfill them.

After eating a bite of lunch, she walked the property. She knew there were ten acres and a thousand feet of shoreline. What she didn't know was how that translated into taxes and income. Behind the buildings were six acres of woods from which her uncle apparently harvested the trees dead or dying of oak wilt. She remembered seeing a chain saw in the

7

storage shed and now she guessed that the other thing on wheels was a wood splitter.

When she returned to the beach, she unlocked the building nearest the water. Sections of pier were stacked inside, along with buoys, cases of two-cycle oil, fishing equipment, two tanks with air pumps which, she guessed, were for minnows, a fridge with a sign that said LEECHES, LEAF WORMS, RED WORMS, NIGHTCRAWLERS. Outside was a gas pump with a gauge and a long hose, which, she assumed, was for filling boat motors. A white raft was pulled up on the beach.

There was no wind today, and the sun warmed her skin. Sitting in the metal chair, she put her thoughts through hoops. Like Jan, she had been city born and raised. Who had helped her uncle with this place? Had he done all the work himself? How would she put in piers, clean cottages, cut and split wood, sell bait, pump gas? She would be forty-seven this summer. Did she really want to work herself to death? Maybe she should reconsider putting the place on the market.

The worry drove her inside to look at her uncle's receipts and expenses. Brochures were heaped in the top drawer of the desk. From Saturday to Saturday a cottage rented for three hundred dollars. The resort was open approximately sixteen weeks. That meant if all units were rented, which they weren't, the income would be around thirty-eight thousand dollars a season. But the tax statement nearly choked her. Real estate taxes were close to fifteen thousand a year, which left twenty-three thousand for maintenance and living expenses. There was no mortgage.

On the other hand, what did she have to lose? She had invested no money. If she couldn't make a go of it or if it was too much work, she would sell. The land itself was worth a fortune. Then she thought of what would disappear from her life — her job with its benefits and Jan. She put down the paperwork and went outside again.

On the way home Sunday, Shelley rehearsed what she'd say to Jan. She was disappointed when Jan's car was gone from its space behind the apartment. Every Sunday Jan went to a Mexican restaurant on the southside to eat with friends. She thought of going there, but she was tired. Lifting the suitcase from her trunk, she carried it inside.

A note on the bed read: *Much to talk about. Be home by seven.* She was encouraged. Falling asleep next to her unpacked bag, she awakened with a start in darkness to the sound of a key in the lock. The clock read nine-fifteen. She got up.

Smelling of other people's cigarettes, Jan stood in the living room. Her graying hair was pulled back in a loose ponytail. She gave Shelley a hug. "How are you, sweetie?" she asked.

"I thought you'd be home," Shelley said.

"You know I go out for Mexican food Sunday night. I thought you'd come there." Jan brushed past her, squeezing her shoulder as she went. "How was the place?"

"Sit down and I'll tell you."

"Let me get ready for bed."

Shelley followed her to the bathroom. "You'd love it, Jan. It's beautiful. Will you come with me next weekend?"

"I've got a meeting on Saturday that I can't miss."

"This is an opportunity of a lifetime."

"Did you put the place on the market?"

"No, Jan. That's what I've been trying to tell you. I want to keep it."

Their eyes met in the reflection of the mirror — Jan's dark, Shelley's gray. "Well, then you'd better find someone to run it soon. It's almost summer."

"I want us to run it," she said, although unable to picture Jan operating a chain saw or splitting wood or selling minnows or cleaning cabins. Maybe she could handle the books and reservations.

Jan was silent as she brushed her teeth, and then said gently, "I told you I won't leave my job or move away from Milwaukee."

"Will you come see the place? Please?" Shelley begged as they climbed into bed.

"All right. I'll drive up next Saturday. Is there somewhere to stay?"

"Yeah. My uncle's house." My house, she thought, no longer able to sit on the excitement. Even though the thought of managing the resort scared her, she knew she wouldn't attempt to sell it. Caught between worry and exhilaration, she lay awake into the small hours.

II

Jan arrived at dusk the following Saturday. Shelley had been waiting since four in the afternoon and was more than a little pissed when Jan's sporty BMW pulled into the sandy driveway. A CPA, Jan earned nearly twice as much as she did as a supervisor at ShopRite. Shelley drove a 1991 Ford Bronco.

"I'd about given you up." The spring peepers, whose offbeat, soprano chorus had filled Shelley's ears all day, were falling silent in the cool evening.

"I'm starved," Jan said.

11

The inside of the house smelled of Shelley's cooking efforts.

"Beans and chicken?" Jan asked as they sat down to eat.

"I had a yen for both." Actually, she'd forgotten to bring potatoes and had found the beans in the cupboard.

Following Jan's gaze around the house, she noticed it looked smaller and darker than when she'd first seen it, even though she'd built a cozy blaze in the fireplace to ferret out the cold mustiness.

"There's a pro-choice rally next Saturday," Jan said. "That's why I was so late. We had to coordinate things and make signs."

Shelley looked at her lover, unable to connect. "I have to be here every day I can get away in order to open at the end of the month." Panic swept over her. She had raked today and picked up branches, dragging them off into the woods on a tarp, but she'd covered at best a half acre. There was still the rest of the grounds to attend to.

"What do I have to do to get a drink around here?"

"Oh, sorry." Opening a bottle of cabernet sauvignon from the supply she'd found under the sink, she poured some into two juice glasses. "Toast."

"To success," Jan said, which Shelley thought was nice.

Light-headed, she wolfed her food and fought off sleep.

"Go lie down, sweetie," Jan said. "You look exhausted. I'll clean up."

* * * * *

12

In the morning the crows, vocalizing loudly outside the windows, wakened Shelley. She couldn't remember Jan coming to bed, and she rolled on an elbow to look at her. She was lying with arms spread and face empty. Jan was tall with a large frame, and her gray hair splayed around her head as if carelessly arranged. Indelible wrinkles fanned outward from her eyes and mouth.

Shelley leaned over and kissed her lips, and Jan's eyes opened. They were the best part of her, dark and full of fire, mirroring her soul. She had worked all her adult life toward a better world for women. Shelley felt regret, then relief, that she wouldn't have time to help her with her quest anymore, and she realized that she was tired of the struggle and wanted out. This was her opportunity.

Jan gave Shelley a wicked grin and reached for her, pulling her like a sack atop where she lay. Shelley felt no desire whatsoever. Instead, a sense of angst overwhelmed her. There was so much to do.

"What is it?" Jan asked.

"Nothing," she replied. "I want to show you the place, is all."

"That can wait a little while, can't it?" Jan coaxed.

"Sure." From her perch Shelley kissed Jan, then slid off to the side and reached between her legs.

"Hey, slow down," Jan murmured.

The knock, followed by a jangling bell, brought them both to their feet where they stood naked on the Southwestern rug. "I'd better go see," Shelley said.

Falling back on the bed, Jan pulled the blanket to her chin. "When I smell the coffee, I'll get up."

Hastily dressed in yesterday's jeans and sweat-shirt, Shelley flung the door open and found herself face-to-face with a large man. Well over six feet and two hundred fifty pounds, he filled the frame. At his side was an immense, black dog — part Labrador, part something unknown. She stepped back.

"Fred Winslow," the man said, thrusting a huge hand at her. "I brought your dog."

"I don't have a dog."

"Sorry about your uncle. This is his dog. Say hello, Hugo."

The dog sat down slowly, like large dogs do, and put a paw on her leg.

She laughed. "I'm Shelley, but I can't take Hugo right now." What was she going to do with such an enormous animal? Their apartment didn't allow pets.

"He can stay with me till you settle in. I help with the outside work, clean up the grounds, mow, fix stuff. It ain't possible to do it all yourself."

"What did my uncle pay you?" she blurted worriedly and then blushed at her audacity.

"Not near enough," he growled, putting a hand out. "Gimme the keys to the storage sheds, and I'll get going."

Meekly, she handed them over and watched him lumber off toward the largest outbuilding. The dog looked back at her before following.

"Who was that?" Jan asked.

She put one hand to her chest. "You scared me."

Jan was peering over her shoulder at Fred's dis-appearing back. "You think you'll be safe here?"

"He said he worked for my uncle. Looks like I inherited the dog along with the resort."

"How do you know he's telling the truth? He

14

could be a mass murderer, using the dog as a ruse. And you gave him the keys."

"Not every man's a killer, Jan," she snapped, annoyed because she'd believed him and was now mistrusting her instincts.

"Why don't you put on the coffee and come back to bed?" Jan said.

"With a murderer in the yard?" How could she make love knowing Fred was just outside?

She left Jan sitting in the kitchen, sipping coffee. A single streak of sunlight bisected her arm and the tabletop.

Fred was piling leaves and branches in a trailer attached to a garden tractor she'd also seen in the storage building. The huge dog blocked her way, barking around a stick in his mouth, his long tail wagging his body.

"He wants you to throw for him," Fred said. "He never gets enough of fetching."

Finding a rake in the unlocked shed, she worked alongside Fred, stopping often to fling sticks for the persistent Hugo, who retrieved immediately and then barked until she threw again.

A brisk breeze blew off the lake, ruffling its surface in the shifting light. Swallows darted over the waves. She was glad that Jan was here to see the place on a sunny day.

They filled two trailers before Jan showed her face. Shelley thought she knew then that nothing here would sway Jan enough to leave Milwaukee, that Jan came to see the resort only to placate her. Cheered anyway by Jan's interest, she leaned her rake against a pine and showed her around.

On the beach, fingers of water reached for their

tennies. Shelley opened the cabins and sheds for Jan to see. Together they explored the woods, shuffling through leaves and tripping over downed trees and branches, the dog crashing ahead. Some of her hope returned.

"Well?"

"It's nice, Shelley. It's lovely. I would love to spend summer vacations here." Jan smiled wistfully, before shrugging. "But I can't leave Milwaukee. I would shrivel up and die."

Stubbornly Shelley said, "I'm going to give notice Monday. I want to give this a try."

Jan put an arm around her and spoke as if she were a child. "I'll tell you what, sweetie. You do this for a year, and I'll come whenever I can."

Shelley leaned into her, missing her already. Jan was familiar, comfortable.

Heading back toward open ground, they grabbed rakes and helped Fred fill the trailer. As she breathed in the smell of lake and pines, Shelley felt an odd mix of happiness and yearning.

"You run a resort before?" Fred said.

"Who, me?" Shelley asked.

"Yeah, ain't you the niece?"

"Yes, and no. I'm a supervisor for ShopRite," she told him, "and Jan is a CPA."

"One of them tax people," he said with a ferocious grin.

"I do taxes for others; I don't collect them." Jan leaned on her rake. Her hair was tied back, the loose ends of the ponytail whipping in the wind.

Shelley shoved her own mostly brown hair out of her face. It was thick and peppered with gray, and she wore it turned under just below her ears. It suited her because she didn't have to mess with it.

"What're you going to do with the place?" he asked.

"Maybe you can teach me the tricks of the trade," she replied. Someone would have to.

He laughed, a loud guffaw that startled her. "You think it's a cinch, I bet."

"I know there's a lot of work."

"You ain't big enough to do some of the things around here." He stopped raking and glared at her. The dog, who had given up the bark and fetch game and was watching nearby, lifted his head from his paws.

"I know," she admitted, wondering why he looked so mad. She had a sneaking suspicion he didn't think a woman was capable of running Pine Shores, that he thought it should be someone like him. Needing his support and knowledge, she said cajolingly, "With your help, I can learn."

At the end of the day she fully understood the phrase *bone-tired*. She realized that the month of May was going to be grueling.

Traffic flowed north on Friday nights, a migration toward the many lakes of central and northern Wisconsin. Shelley joined the stream of cars as soon as her five o'clock shift ended. When she turned west off Highway 41, the sun was low enough to nearly blind her. A deer leaped out of the ditch and bounded over the road, followed by two others. Slamming on the brakes, she missed the last animal only by driving onto the gravel berm. Her heart thrummed in her throat, her legs turned into wet noodles. She drove carefully on.

Turning the Bronco into the drive that was marked by a three-by-five-foot wood sign, she wound through the dark pines to the house and eight cabins and the lake beyond. The night sounds flowed over her — the peepers and frogs, the lake brushing against the shore, a motorboat sputtering to life. Otherwise, there was silence.

Unlocking the door to the house and flooding the rooms with light, she carried her suitcase and the bags of groceries and staples inside. Jan would come tomorrow. Tonight she was on her own. She ate and read and went to bed.

Up with the early light, she looked over what Fred had accomplished during the week. The grounds were swept clean. Walking to the metal chair, coffee cup in hand, she sat on its cool seat. A heron was stabbing food in the shallows.

She watched Fred drive in and walk toward her. Grizzled whiskers framed his mouth, making him appear more menacing than ever. With delighted bounds, Hugo reached her first. The dog licked her face, then splashed into the lake, fracturing the water into prisms. Letting out a squawk, the heron flapped heavily into the air.

"The place looks nice," she said.

He grunted. "We still got lots to do. Them cabins need work."

"I'm ready." She stood and set her empty coffee cup on the chair.

Most of the day she ran for nails and boards and

guttering, and tossed sticks for Hugo while awaiting Fred's next command. When Jan arrived late in the afternoon, he was taking a beer break down by the water.

"Well, just in time," Fred growled. "Ain't you girls partners?"

"Not in this venture," Jan said, wincing at the word *girls*.

When Fred left, rattling out in his old Dodge half-ton truck with the dog balanced precariously on the front seat, Shelley asked Jan why she hadn't told Fred they weren't girls.

"I'm so far from being a girl that it's either laughable or flattering."

"You're mellowing, Jan."

"That's what aging does."

The heron was back, blending into the backdrop of bushy growth. Pine Shores bordered the west end of the lake where a swamp drained off the overflow. The frogs' evening serenade was being choked off by the nightly drop in temperature.

"Pretty, huh?" Shelley nodded toward clouds laced with reds and purples, framed against the darkening blue of the sky.

"Lovely, but I'm chilled, sweetie," Jan said. "Why don't we go inside and make supper?"

They puttered around the kitchen, a familiar scene. "Fixing dinner with you is comforting. Do you know that?"

Jan pulled the cork from a bottle of merlot. "That's nice, Shelley. But I can't spend every weekend here. This is going to be a time of separation."

"I'm scared to death, Jan," she admitted. "What if I can't make a go of it?"

19

"Come home. I'll be there. It's like you said. You can't lose anything but a year of your time."

At one the next day, Fred's pickup clattered into the yard, trailing thick exhaust. "Get your suits on, ladies," he called, as close to merriment as he'd yet come. Hugo, tongue lolling, leaped out of the open truck window and rushed toward them.

They had just finished eating lunch and were standing in the yard, indecisive as to what to tackle next. Shelley patted the large dog, who brought her a stick.

"Looks like a good day to put in the pier." Fred grinned, showing off long, yellow teeth. Smiling only rearranged the contours of his face. He still looked slightly dissolute and dangerous.

When they were knee deep in icy water, Jan spoke through clenched jaws. "Maybe we should wait for warmer weather." She wore shorts and an ancient T-shirt, and whenever she looked at Shelley, she laughed.

Shelley felt she couldn't complain, though, as she stood in an old swimsuit she'd found in a box in the storage closet. Someone must have left it behind. Its yellow-and-pink floral design crawled up her ass and bagged at her breasts. It was bad enough to be shivering in the lake without the added insult of looking like a fool.

The dog, on the other hand, romped joyously through the shallows, sending water flying. They cringed whenever he came near.

She glanced away from Fred, who was white from the neck down and whose belly bulged obscenely over his Hawaiian shorts. A network of black hair covered him. "Just get the pier out of the shed for me," he growled.

She and Jan dutifully carried the sections from the building to the beach, while Fred set up the frame and adjusted it in the water. When he was waist deep, a motorboat drove past. Its wake washed over his large belly. "Goddamn son of a bitch. Slow down," he hollered, waving a crescent wrench at the offending boat. Lumbering out of the lake, he put the wood sections on the frame and changed into clothes in the building, while she went with Jan to the house. Once there, they collapsed with laughter.

When they left for Milwaukee around five, Fred was gone, promising to mow the grass and finish what outside repairs were needed. Next weekend was Memorial Day. She'd have to race toward the lake at five, which was the earliest she could leave. Bill Hailey and Ted were due to arrive that evening for the holiday. She had promised to work through the first week of June. On June eighth the weekly reservations would begin.

III

The Friday of Memorial Day weekend, Shelley noticed the car parked near cabin eight as soon as she drove in. She found the two men standing on the pier, one sighting through a scope on a tripod.

The other offered his hand. "I'm Bill. This is Ted Dzabo." He patted Ted on the back. "You must be Shelley."

"I'm sorry I couldn't be here when you arrived," she said. "I still work in Milwaukee."

"Take a peek." Ted stepped away from the scope.

The great blue heron stood caught in the glass. "Amazing." She saw every marking, the blink of its eye before its beak shot toward the water and impaled a minnow.

Bill was short and slight with thinning brown hair and kind eyes of a nondescript brown. Broad-shouldered and thickly built, Ted was taller, a jock who'd lost his tone. Dimples made him look cherubic.

She gave them the key to their cottage and said proudly, "You're my first guests."

A smile transformed Bill's face. "I'm so glad you're not going to sell the place. It would probably be split up and developed."

"Well, we'll see how the year goes." After all, this was a trial run. She wasn't promising anything.

"We asked for number eight because of the wetlands," he explained. "They're always full of birds."

"And frogs," she said. The amphibians' passion was sometimes deafening.

"Aren't they wonderful," Ted said.

"Yes," she agreed. "I hope they don't keep you awake."

The next morning she heard the first bird before five. At seven she gave up attempting to sleep and took her coffee to the pier, carrying the metal chair with her.

Bill was already there, peering through the scope.

"See anything?" she asked.

"Sure. Look."

She set her cup down and took a brief peek. As big as life, a gaudy wood duck flew out of a nesting box, landing on the water below. "Wow."

"It's a good time of year to bird. Not so many

23

people or boats around." He gave her a sweet smile as she relinquished the scope. "Your uncle was a great guy."

"I wish I'd known him. I've met Fred."

He laughed. "Fred's okay. He was Scott's right hand after Phil died."

"He's been a godsend. Who was Phil?"

"Your uncle's partner."

"Oh." She stared at the lake. The weekend was beginning on a promising note — blue sky, scattered white clouds, a slight breeze stirring the water. Feeling the heat of the sun, she resisted the urge to run to the house for her sunblock. "What was he like?"

"Your uncle or Phil?"

"My uncle."

"Kind, generous. Whenever he had the time, he loved to sit on the dock and read."

"You'd have to be a reader to spend a winter here, or a TV watcher." And he hadn't been a television fan, because there was no satellite dish.

Ted carried two cups of coffee onto the pier. Handing one to Bill, he bent to look in the scope at the wood duck box. "Seen any ducklings?"

She stood and stretched. "Time to get going. I'll see you later."

"Hey, what'd I do?" Ted asked.

"Nothing. My coffee's gone."

"I'll get you some," Bill offered.

"No, thanks. I have to eat and do something constructive. See you both later."

That day she cleaned three more cabins while Ted and Bill helped Fred put in the rest of the dock and float the raft. She heard their bantering shouts and

24

Fred's loud directions whenever she stepped outside. The ice was only recently gone from the far northern lakes, and except for last weekend, they'd had an unusually cold spring.

When Jan arrived late in the day, Shelley was sharing Bill and Ted's cocktail hour on the elongated pier. They had set three lawn chairs at the T-end and she, at least, was feeling pleasantly mellow. She introduced Jan to the men.

Ted left to fix Jan a drink, while Bill went in search of a chair.

Jan stared at the rippling lake. "Has the water warmed up any?"

"I don't know. Bill and Ted helped Fred with the rest of the pier."

"You have the guests working?" Jan inspired guilt. "God, what a day. I went to the office this morning and then cleaned the apartment before driving here. I don't know if I can do this many weekends."

The two men returned, and Ted handed Jan a martini.

"Thanks." She slapped at a mosquito. "Nothing like being right next to a swamp."

"Wetlands," Bill said gently.

"Do you have any Off! insect repellant?" she asked.

Shelley tossed her a stick of Cutters.

Later when they were alone, Jan said, "If I want to be eaten alive, I'll ask you to do it. They are nice guys, though. How'd they get along with Fred?"

"It sounded like a good time." She was thinking about the next day and all there was to do.

* * * * *

Shelley had installed an answering machine in her uncle's house, and there was a flurry of phone messages from people wanting to make reservations. She took charge card numbers over the phone and checks through the mail. Next weekend three cabins would be occupied. The following Saturday four were reserved for the week. She couldn't wait for work to end. ShopRite had never looked so drab.

Shelley cleaned the remaining four cabins over the next two days; Fred checked out the motors in storage; and Jan planted flowers around the house and rental cottages. Bill and Ted lazed on the dock and took long walks.

Sunday evening Ted and Bill invited the women to dinner. Before dinner, Bill mixed drinks and Ted produced a tray with hummus and pita bread, black bean dip and baked chips, and a small bottle of Beano tablets. A smile lit his face.

Jan laughed. "You've thought of everything."

The meal became raucous early on.

When Shelley told a penguin joke, walking around in imitation of one, she realized someone was standing outside the porch. Slightly tipsy with drink and mirth, she went to the door.

A woman stood in the yard. "Hi. Do you have a phone I could use?" Scrapes on the woman's cheek and forehead welled with blood.

"What happened?" Shelley let the screen door slam behind her.

"I ran into a tree where the road curves. A deer jumped out in front of me." The woman's smile was as distracted as her eyes. She looked a little crazy.

"You're hurt."

Jan and the two men joined them on the sandy grass.

"She needs to use the phone," Shelley said.

Bill and Ted quickly moved to either side of the woman, supporting her as she stumbled.

"Better run ahead and call 911," Bill said to Jan and Shelley.

"No. I'm fine," the woman protested. "Really."

"We'll take you to emergency."

"I can't afford it."

"You can't afford not to," Ted insisted.

"I have to get my car off that tree. Maybe if I could just lie down for a while."

"We'll take care of the car."

They were carrying her by her arms toward the house, where they deposited her on the couch. Bill bent over and gently opened one eye wide.

"Do you have medical training?" Jan asked as they stood around the wood-framed sofa.

"Some," he said.

It occurred to Shelley that she could benefit from a course in emergency care. At least, she wouldn't feel so helpless as she did now.

"You keep quiet now," Ted said to the woman. "We'll rescue your car."

The woman tried to sit up. "I left my wallet and keys in it."

"We'll get them," Bill promised, gently pushing her down. "Don't worry."

Her eyes closed in a face so pale that Shelley was frightened. "Would you like some water?"

"Do you have any aspirin? I've got a pounding headache."

27

Shelley and Jan looked at each other, and Jan shook her head.

"I don't think you should take anything till you see a doctor."

Shelley was trying to recall the color of the woman's eyes. Her hair was a dishwater blond, a thick cap framing high cheek bones, a straight nose, light-colored brows, and curling lashes shadowing oval eyelids.

"My name's Emily," she murmured.

Was it okay for someone with a head injury to sleep? Shelley didn't know. Again she looked at Jan for instruction.

Jan mouthed, "Call the ER."

A doctor from ER said to bring her in, and Jan told Shelley in the kitchen that they couldn't risk otherwise. They waited impatiently for Ted and Bill.

When the men returned towing a battered Geo, they placed Emily in the backseat of Jan's BMW, undoubtedly the smoothest driving vehicle on hand, and convoyed her to the hospital.

IV

Friday arrived and once again Shelley was on the road at five P.M., joining the northward weekend migration. The drive stretched before her monotonously. She thought of Jan, who was staying home. But her disappointment was encased in a wider span of excitement as she sped toward the lake and the anticipation of new guests.

The mailbox at the end of the resort driveway yielded a letter. She tore it open.

Dear Shelley and Jan,

Thanks for being so caring last weekend. I'm home, I'm well. I'll stop to see you on Saturday. I'd like to get Ted and Bill's addresses, so that I can write to them.

Sincerely,

Emily Hodson

How nice, she thought, stepping into the sounds of nature that she found so relaxing. Maybe it was her imagination, but she thought the night was quieter. The occasional deep-throated call of the bullfrogs had replaced the soprano of the chorus variety, and the peepers were silent. She'd miss them when they had finally spent all their reproductive energy. A motorboat growled on the lake.

Before she could change clothes, the first guests arrived. Parking their dark green Ford Explorer at cabin one, the two men sauntered toward her with the assurance that comes with good looks. Both were tall and muscular with thick hair and square jaws; they were enough to make straight women cry. Was it true that gay men stay in shape longer than their heterosexual counterparts? But then she thought of Ted and Bill.

Introducing themselves as Jason and Shawn, their white-toothed smiles made her want to check her own in the mirror.

"We like to get as far away from the mosquitoes as possible," Jason said, when she handed him the key to the cabin. "Anyone else coming this weekend?"

"Cabins three and six are reserved." Mentally, she ticked off what she had to do over the next two days. Clean number eight and dust two, four, six, and seven for the following weekend. She'd always hated cleaning, but she couldn't afford to hire someone to help.

Fred had mowed. Paying him was biting into her savings, but he took care of the grounds and buildings and kept the machinery running. She had permission from the court to run the resort, had notified the credit card companies of the change in management, had started a checking account in her name, but the estate wasn't settled. She didn't have access to her uncle's money.

The other renters knocked on the door as she unbagged groceries. The four men looked like weight lifters; the three women had to be jocks. Had her uncle rented to any straight people? She grinned as she gave them their keys, sending the men to number three, nearest the other guys, and the women to six.

Desperately wanting a little time to herself, she poured a glass of wine and carried it and a lawn chair toward the pier.

Jason and Shawn caught up with her. "There's nothing in the boat, not even a motor."

"I know," she said. "I can give you everything else. Fred will be here in the morning to put the motors on."

"We could do that," Jason volunteered

She unlocked the storage shed. "Sorry. I don't know which are ready to use. We'll have to wait for Fred."

The men went off with oars and life jackets and cushions, and she returned to her glass of wine on the dock. It was getting dark, she was hungry, and the mosquitoes were out. Bats flitted overhead, dipping and soaring. She knew they ate mosquitoes, but she ducked anyway whenever one came close.

A screen door slammed, and the women made their way toward her. When they stepped on the pier, she sighed.

"How's the water?" She knew their names, but she didn't know which matched what face.

"Cold, I expect," she said, giving up hope of privacy. On the way back to the house, she passed cabin three where the four guys were partying on their front porch.

Later, the men in that cabin tested the water, shouting and laughing into the night until the others joined them. Going outside, she found them all splashing in the dark.

They called to her. "Come on in. It's so cold you can't feel a thing."

The full moon and thousands of stars floated on the expanse of black water that began at her feet.

The next morning Fred put the motors on three boats. "You gotta mix the gas and oil. I'll show you," he said. "Scott used to do it himself and put it in five-gallon cans. You can't trust them people to take care of what's yours. I don't care what they say." He started each motor with a pull and took test drives around the lake. Hugo rode in the bow, his ears jutting in the breeze.

Shading her eyes, she watched from the dock.

She'd been wakened by pounding on the door before seven.

"Got a plunger?" one of the men in cabin three had asked, his face a deep red.

"I'll look." Shuffling off, trying in vain to stay asleep, she'd found one in the bathroom closet.

The sky was thinly veiled, the air cool. She felt somehow responsible for the weather. However, the guests behaved as if it were midsummer and hot. They buzzed around the lake in the boats and swam and played catch. They were not as quiet as Bill and Ted had been.

Late afternoon, when she stepped out of cabin seven, she noticed the Geo with its bent fender and twisted bumper parked behind her Bronco. Emily was standing on the front stoop of the house.

"How are you doing?" Shelley met her halfway.

Emily's eyes were a shading of blue and gray and were neither large nor small. Everything was in perspective, as if she'd been carefully put together.

"Fine, thanks to you and the others." Emily gestured at her small vehicle. "I can't say that about my car, though."

"Come on in," Shelley said, remembering why Emily was here. "I'll write down Ted and Bill's address for you."

"Where's Jan?"

"In Milwaukee." In the corner of the living room was the desk. Paging through the address book, she jotted the information down. She asked, more for something to say, "So, what do you do around here?"

Most of the jobs in the area were seasonal and tourist related.

"Nothing yet. I haven't been here long. My dad died and I moved back to be with my mother." Folding the paper, Emily pocketed it in her jeans.

"I'm sorry," Shelley said, recalling her own parents' deaths. She had felt cheated, losing them just when she was beginning to really know them. She had been a late baby; her brothers were ten and eight years older.

Emily looked briefly away. "It was very sudden."

She waited to hear more.

"If you need any help, let me know." Emily offered a warm smile. "I owe you."

"Thanks, but you don't owe me anything."

"Yes, I do."

She thought of the weekly headlong rush to beat the arriving guests. "All right. Can you be here next Friday afternoon around five to open cabins?" Some of the guests had asked to come early since the cabins were unoccupied.

Realizing next week would be her last afternoon drive from Milwaukee, and experiencing a heady blend of relief and excitement, she asked, "Would you like to have a glass of wine with me?"

"Sure."

They walked to the dock. The guests were out in the motorboats, taking an evening cruise around the lake, well warmed, she was sure, by drink. "I like to begin and end the days here like this." A weak sun barely filtered the clouds, wrapping the sky in gray.

When Emily left soon after, saying that her mother was expecting her home for dinner, Shelley looked in the fridge for something to eat. Jan was the cook in the family. A knock on the door interrupted her.

Tucked into a hooded sweatshirt, Shawn's grin was boyish. "We're grilling out. Want to join us?"

"Sounds good," she said, pulling on a heavy jacket.

A fire roared in the outdoor fireplace. Brats and hamburgers sizzled on portable grills nearby, away from the fierce blaze that was providing heat to this group of cheerful young people determined to enjoy a bad weather weekend.

Shelley's son, Joe, had called the apartment on Saturday while she was at the lake and had asked Jan to tell his mother to ring him back. Once a month Shelley called him, but she came away from their phone conversation feeling bereft. The rift created when she'd left his dad couldn't be closed with words, and she was tired of being verbally slapped for what had happened six years ago.

"Was he rude?" she asked Jan.

"No. He was looking for work this summer. Thought maybe you could use him."

"I can't afford him," she said. "But I could give him room and board." Joe was in graduate school. He'd been a freshman at the university, already gone from home himself, when she'd moved out. "I'll call him tomorrow," she decided.

When she did call the next night, she was pleasantly surprised by his friendliness. She almost succumbed to it and offered him work. But then she would have to pay him as well as Fred; Fred was her mainstay; she couldn't pay them both.

"I have all the help I can afford, Joey." She quickly added, "I can put you up, though. Maybe you can find work in the area."

"Okay," he said, still cheerful.

Why her, why now, she wanted to ask. Why didn't he work for his dad as he had in the past? His father was an electrical contractor. But all she said was, "It'll be wonderful to have you." He hadn't stayed with her since she'd gone her separate way.

"When can I come?" he asked.

"How about next weekend?" She gave him directions.

"How'd it go?" Jan asked.

"He's spending the summer with me," she said, hardly able to believe it.

"It's about time. I'm glad." Jan squeezed her hand, apparently not questioning Joe's motives as she was doing.

In the beginning Shelley had thought she understood her son's slights, his sullenness when he was forced to talk to her. She was patient with him, understanding that she'd broken up the family home, stepped out of the accustomed role of mother and wife, and made Joe unwillingly responsible for his dad's happiness. She was sure he would outgrow his anger. Perhaps he felt she'd rejected him too. What she'd wondered later was whether he was threatened by her homosexuality, because it made him face his own same-sex orientation.

But when she'd questioned his continuing rejection, he'd said, "You left Dad for *her*," in a tone full of rage.

He wasn't referring to Jan. Shelley hadn't met her yet. What he meant was that she'd left a long-term marriage for a woman she barely knew, one who was catting around on her already — although that he couldn't have known.

The ensuing silence between them had stretched until the woman left her.

V

Shelley spent the week packing and shopping. Wednesday after work, some of her coworkers took her out for a farewell dinner. In her mind she was already gone; she only regretted having to leave Jan. However, Jan was going with her this first weekend, carrying Shelley's clothing in the BMW so she could load the Bronco with toilet paper, paper towels, and cleaning supplies from Sam's Club.

Arriving around seven-thirty, they found Joe and Emily chatting on the stoop. Shelley had been frantic, forced to wait for Jan who worked till five-thirty, hoping that Emily had everything under control — which she did.

As Joe wrapped Shelley in a hug, Emily helped Jan carry in the bagged supplies and loads of clothing.

"Nice place, Mom," he said with a winning smile. At five feet, ten inches, he had the lean muscles of a wrestler or swimmer. His build and sand-colored hair and eyes reminded her of his father in his youth. "I didn't know I had an Uncle Scott."

"He was not what you'd call a close relative. How are you, Joey?"

He blinked. "Fine, Mom. And you?"

Maybe they could start fresh. "Good. Excited." An ancient, rusting Honda was parked next to Emily's damaged Geo. She assumed it was his. "Bring your stuff inside."

He slung a backpack over his shoulder and a duffle bag under his arm. The two bedrooms branched off a short hall, as did the bathroom. The room at the far end faced the woods.

"How's your father?"

Setting his belongings on the bed, he avoided her eyes and poked at the braided rug with a foot. "He's fine. Um, actually he's living with someone."

"Have you met her?"

He nodded. "Yeah. She's okay. Kind of young, but hey."

Now she understood why he was here. Turning away, she smiled.

She told Jan in bed that night, "I think he's ready to make amends."

"What is he now? Twenty-four? It's about time."

"I suppose he feels like he's losing his dad too and doesn't want to lose us both."

"When I was his age, I was out in the world earning a living."

"Give him a chance, Jan. He was polite."

Jan turned her back. "Why wouldn't he be? It's high time he stopped behaving like a brat."

"He's an only child. I suppose we spoiled him," she whispered, surprised by Jan's criticism.

"Make him help you, Shelley."

"I will," she promised.

The next day, she opened the door to summer and what she mistook as freedom. Thinking she'd have her coffee on the front porch, she stretched in the fresh morning air. Hugo sat up from his bed on the outside step and looked at her accusingly. Remembering that he was her dog now, she opened the screen for him.

"When did you get here?" she asked, running a hand over his coat and smelling something vile. Leaning over, she sniffed behind his ear. "Out." Opening the screen again, she pointed.

He tucked his tail and slunk back onto the stoop.

Rousing Joe from sleep, she said, "There's a fish somewhere that needs burying, and the dog has to have a bath."

"What dog?" He stood in his open doorway, his hair on end, dressed in boxer shorts.

"Hugo. I inherited him too." She turned away. "The coffee's on."

He pulled on jeans and stumbled outside with a bar of soap. He leaned over Hugo. "Phew! Come on, fella. Bath time."

Watching them walk toward the lake, she recalled how he had loved their family dogs. He'd taken his first steps clinging to their retriever. When they'd bought another pup after the first dog died, it had gone everywhere possible with him.

A man and woman were striding purposefully toward the house from cabin seven. She hadn't met any of the guests who'd arrived yesterday. *Uh-oh,* she thought as they drew close, instinctively knowing something was amiss.

The man's round face peered at her through the screen. "Are you the owner?"

Stepping outside, she closed the door quietly. The grass was wet and spiky. "Yes. I'm Shelley."

"We didn't get any sleep last night. The people in the next cabin partied until morning."

She hadn't heard them and said so.

The woman's voice, already pitched high, rose a decibel. "They were swimming at three A.M."

"I'll talk to them," she promised, "or you can move to one of the unoccupied cabins."

"What's up?" Jan asked from the porch as the couple marched back to their cabin.

"I can't afford to give them their money back," she said, going inside to pour more coffee.

"Part of the job is keeping the guests happy, sweetie. They come here with different expectations."

41

She thought wistfully of the group last weekend and how they had partied together joyously. She wasn't looking forward to talking to the guests in cabin eight. Their expectations obviously were not of a reclusive nature.

It was not an auspicious beginning. The moon-faced couple left in the afternoon, paying only one day's rent. She watched them drive out in a flurry of sand. Everyone else was on or near the water, waiting for the predictable laser of hot sunshine to beam down between high-flying clouds. Hugo lay in the shallows, occasionally lapping at the wavelets, worn out finally after hours of retrieving for the little boys in cabin two.

Jan read on the dock. Joe lay sunning on the raft with the men from cabins four and eight. Fred was keeping an eye on the boat landing, his chair tilted back.

Discouraged at losing a week's rent, she went inside to answer the phone.

"Hi, it's Emily." She sounded hesitant.

"What's up?"

"Nothing much. I'm bored."

"Well, come on over then. Join the sun worshipers."

"Is it okay?"

"Of course."

When Emily arrived, she sat on the pier and dangled her feet in the water.

Shelley stood looking at the lake, which was alternately bright and dark as the clouds swept overhead. She was thinking that if the couple had just waited a

little, it would have been quiet enough even for
them. Just then shouts rose from the raft. One of
the guys was floating a cooler of beer out.

"Want a Lite?" Joe held up a bottle toward the
dock. They shook their heads in unison. He raised it
higher. "What about you, Fred?"

"Sure," Fred said, and Joe swam one in for him.
Even the parents of the little boys accepted his offer.

"Is it cocktail hour already?" Jan asked, looking
at her watch. "Four o'clock. I'll mix."

"None for me," Shelley said.

When evening arrived, the guests built a fire in
the outdoor fireplace. The little boys roasted marshmallows and fed half of theirs to Hugo. Their parents
hauled them off to bed around ten. By midnight
everyone had gone to their cabins, except Shelley. She
walked the grounds like a wraith, slapping at
mosquitoes, as Hugo plodded behind. Clouds had
blotted out the stars.

Tomorrow Jan would leave, and she'd be on her
own.

Hugo's persistent barking woke Shelley Sunday
morning. A truck and trailer were rattling down the
driveway. Dragging herself from Jan's side, she pulled
on shorts and a T-shirt and went out into a dewy
morning.

"The early bird gets the worm. I hope you got
some for sale."

Only a fisherman could be so cheerful at six in

the morning, she thought as she grunted affirma-
tively. He unloaded his bass boat and handed her ten
bucks. Lined up waiting were two other trucks and
trailers. She was forced to pee in the bushes during a
brief respite.

The morning was cool and quiet, except for the
birds. The smells of lake and pines, of junipers and
sweet clover, blended to produce a heady fragrance.
Sitting on the chair where Fred had been yesterday,
she soaked up the first rays of sun. She'd have to
put a coffeepot in the building, along with the bait,
she decided.

Hugo wagged a greeting to Joe, who appeared
quietly at her side carrying a cup of coffee. "Thought
you might need this."

"Thanks." She smiled up at him, the sun in her
eyes. His sandy hair glowed.

"Why didn't you wake me?"

"I was up anyway."

"You can go eat breakfast now," he said.

Were Mondays always so quiet? Joe was job
hunting and Fred hadn't arrived. Over the weekend
speedboats careened around the lake, towing water
skiers. The buzzing of Jet Skis, added to the noise.
The lake became a giant playground for pleasure
seekers. Apparently, most of them had packed up
Sunday night and left for home.

Jan was gone. Maybe that was causing Shelley
her melancholy. They had made perfunctory love
Sunday morning after Joe took watch over the boat
ramp. It had left her unsatisfied, and she suspected
that Jan had felt the same. She wasn't sure their

44

relationship would survive this separation. Perhaps Jan thought that too.

Sitting on the porch with a cup of coffee, she felt the lake's magnetic pull. She hadn't yet cleaned cabin seven. Grabbing sheets and fresh towels, she went outside. Hugo was stretched out in the concave hollow she had scolded him for digging in the sandy yard. He got up to follow, his tail wagging in friendly greeting.

She had talked to the men in cabin eight about their partying. She'd found them charming and apologetic. She suspected that the moonfaced couple had been displeased in other ways.

The little boys shouted for Hugo, who ran toward them with joyous abandon. There were no signs of life from the other cabins. It was early, only eight.

When she finished cleaning, she dumped the laundry on the cabin porch and walked to the dock. A no-wake rule was in effect from ten to five, and only a handful of fishing boats dotted the water. Ragged wisps of fog rose like ghosts off the lake's surface.

The pier moved slightly. She turned with a ready smile and was surprised to see Emily.

Emily's face was flushed. "Thought you might need a friend today."

"How did you know?"

"I guessed." She shrugged

"Would you like a cup of coffee?"

"If you have time."

They sat on the screened-in porch. She'd found that she had more privacy there. The parents in cabin two took chairs to the beach to watch the little boys play in the water with Hugo. Cabins four and eight showed no signs of life. Shelley had heard their occupants last night as she tossed and turned in bed. Faint laughter had drifted in the open window.

Only three cabins were rented. She would have to revise her estimated income. Next week, though, six were reserved, and starting the last week in June they were booked solid until after Labor Day weekend. She thought how it would be, getting everything ready for incoming guests. There'd be no time then for a leisurely cup of coffee.

"How is it going?" Emily asked. "Do you need more help?"

"Not yet," she said.

"I'll be glad to pitch in."

Shelley smiled. "Thanks, but you'll probably have a job by then."

"I do now. I start tomorrow."

"What? Where?"

"At the bank in town." Emily grinned at her. "I know. Boring."

Realizing she knew very little about Emily, she said, "Where did you live before you moved back here?"

Fred's truck drove in and died in a clatter of noise.

"Madison. I worked at a bank there too." Emily smiled and shrugged.

"Ho, ladies. Did you order more bait, Shell?" It was Fred's good-mood name for her. He stood just outside the screen, his hands buried in the pockets of his ragged shorts. The bottom button of his shirt was open, revealing a hint of hairy belly.

"Yep. It's supposed to arrive today."

"I'll clean out the tank. Most of them minnows

46

are floating belly-up. Got to split some wood too."
Nearly every night someone lit a fire in the outdoor
fireplace.

When Fred ambled off toward the boat ramp,
Hugo was streaking through the grounds toward him.

Shelley laughed softly. "I always want to howl
when he wears shorts. I don't know why."

"I should go," Emily said. "I've got a ton of
things to do."

"You just got here," she protested.

"I'll come back some evening. How does that
sound?"

"Good. Maybe we can finally have a conversation."

VI

The storage building leaked. It had poured the night before, a drenching rain, and the inside of Shelley's bass boat was soaked. The place smelled musty. Pools of water had collected on the floor.

"Needs a new roof, Shell," Fred grunted.

"How much will that cost?" she asked worriedly.

"Don't know. Materials. I can do it with Joe's help, and yours." His grin came and went so quickly she wondered whether she had seen it.

She'd gone over the books that morning. It was July and all the cabins were occupied, yet somehow the money drained away. She felt frantic most of the time, rushing from one thing to another.

"You said the cabins need reroofing." The dog leaned against her leg, warm and solid. She rested a hand on his ruff, and he pressed himself closer.

"Maybe they'll wait till spring."

There wouldn't be any more money in the spring. She knew that.

Joey had taken a job supplying propane to customers with the local gas company. When he was home he made himself useful, but he worked six days a week. Shelley wished she could afford to pay him to work for her.

She had gone to First National shortly after Emily started working there and was directed to one of the glass-paned rooms.

"You have your own office?" she asked, feeling inexplicably annoyed and foolish that Emily hadn't told her she was a loan officer. She had expected to see her behind a teller's window.

Emily nodded dismissively, and then said, "I'm off weekends. I'll still come over Saturday mornings to help."

Shelley fought the urge to say she didn't need any help. She did. Saturdays were frantic with rentees departing, followed by the rush to clean cabins for the new guests. Emily had offered a hand in June. When Shelley tried to pay her, she said the use of the grounds was payment enough.

* * * * *

It was cool for the third week in July, Shelley thought as she cleaned a cabin while Emily changed the sheets. Fred's hammering could be heard over the noise of the Hoover. She was expecting Jan in the afternoon. She hadn't seen her in two weeks, yet she worried that Jan would only slow her down. Saturdays were her busiest days.

Carrying the vacuum to the last cabin, she glanced toward the beach where the new guests were gathering. Anxiety nagged her. There had to be a better way to check out and in. This desperate race to ready the cabins for afternoon arrivals was taking its toll. Maybe the guests should bring their own sheets and do their own cleaning. Most of them did tidy up before leaving, washing dishes and sweeping floors. She hadn't thought she'd be a maid.

When they finished the last cabin, she took care of the reservations, apologizing for the inconvenience. Bill Hailey and Ted Dzabo waited their turn. Emily stood talking to them on the porch. When the remaining guests were gone, Shelley joined them.

"I'd forgotten you were coming this week." She was surprised at how pleased she was by their presence.

"We just told Emily that we're looking for a place on a lake to buy. Year-round." Bill beamed as he winked at her. "Think you could stand us as neighbors?"

Her every thought focused on money these days — she would lose them as paying guests. But she only said, "You'll brighten my winter."

Ted jumped in enthusiastically. "The county needs

a psychologist; they offered me the job. It means less pay, but we expected that. And Bill wants to sell antiques."

Bill, she knew, was an attorney. He probably could afford to retire. For a moment she envied them their freedom to choose. But she had chosen. Her uncle had given her the chance. She briefly worried that she would let him down, that the costs of running the resort would exceed its income.

She and Emily walked with them to cabin eight, commenting on the changes eight weeks had wrought. From the wetlands came the chirring of insects and the occasional chunk of a frog. The redwing blackbirds that nested in its tall grasses were flocking now. The heron flapped across the lake, its long legs trailing.

"It's good to be back," Bill said. "We want both of you to come for dinner tomorrow night. And Jan, of course."

Shelley realized that Jan would probably have come and gone by then. She glanced over her shoulder reflexively, looking in vain for the BMW. "What can I bring?" she asked.

"Yourselves. Ted has a new recipe to try out on you."

Emily smiled, her hands in the back pockets of her shorts. "Thanks."

Jan arrived after four, and she and Joe talked nonstop through dinner, fueling each other's questions. Shelley said little and listened less. When she realized that Jan was staring at her, she straightened.

"Did I miss something?"

"Did you hear anything?" Jan asked.

"Bill and Ted are here. They invited us to dinner tomorrow, Jan."

Jan shook her head. "I can't. I have to work Monday."

She told Jan that the two men were looking for a place to buy on a lake, that they were moving. "You could work in the area too. There's always a job for a CPA," she said, hearing the wistfulness in her voice.

But Jan shook her head. "I'll go see them in the morning."

Joe glanced from Jan to her. "I'm going out tonight. Take in a movie, do a little dancing."

Caught by surprise, she said, "Be careful."

"Yeah, Ma, you too."

"You'll be drinking and driving and —" She flared back, finding she couldn't finish the sentence. He was a grown man, after all.

"And fucking? Is that what you were going to say? Just to set your mind at ease, I have a pocketful of condoms. See?" He pulled out a handful and showed them to her. They glowed in different colors.

Her face grew hot, although Jan was grinning.

And Joe smiled. "You look like a tomato, Mom. Don't worry. If I drink too much, I'll stay in town. Excuse me now." A few minutes later they heard the shower.

"How can anyone take a fluorescent orange or green prick seriously?" she asked.

Jan burst into laughter. "I was wondering that myself."

When Joe left, she asked, "What's going on, Shelley? I don't think you heard a word of what was said during dinner."

"Preoccupied." She sighed loudly. "The income barely keeps up with the expenses, Jan. Something is always in need of repair. Why does everything boil down to money? My uncle probably worried himself to death."

"You look like you've lost weight." Jan smiled at her. "Are you going to show me how much?"

"Later." Someone was lighting an early fire in the outdoor fireplace. Others were swimming or boating or fishing. She wasn't ready for bed yet. Sex was not a priority right now, which surprised her.

Jan said, "Okay, sweetie. I understand. Want to take a walk? Go see Ted and Bill?"

But Ted and Bill's car was gone.

It was dusk when they returned to the house, having gone to the dock first and the fire afterward, where Hugo stayed behind — someone always shared marshmallows with him.

"How's Emily anyway?" Jan said.

"Fine. She'll be over tomorrow."

"She's an attractive woman."

"Do you think she's a lesbian?" They were standing by the bed, peeling off their clothes.

"I know she is." Jan threw back the covers. Her full breasts dangled as she bent over the bed.

Shelley felt a stir of desire. "How can you tell?" She reached to touch the soft flesh.

"Hey, that tickles." Jan covered the breast with one hand. "Trust me, I know."

53

"Lesbian vibes?" She cupped the uncovered breast, eliciting a giggle. It made her smile.

Jan pulled her down on the bed and rolled on top of her. "You're a tease, sweetie."

"Am I?" She didn't think of herself that way. When she was ready for sex, she went for it.

But Jan was through talking. Her tongue was in Shelley's mouth, her hand between Shelley's legs. Surprised by the passion, Shelley lagged behind. Jan was kissing her eyelids, her neck, her breasts, pulling the desire out of her with long fingers and spreading it around.

When Shelley began panting, Jan slipped to the side so that she could be reached. It was all over quickly.

"What brought that on?" she asked.

"The thought of losing you," Jan replied.

"I'm not that easy to get rid of."

"I think this place is stealing you away."

Shelley wondered.

They went to see Ted and Bill in the morning. The sun was already beating its golden path across the lake. The four of them sat on cabin eight's front porch and drank coffee.

"There seems to be a general exodus toward the lakes," Jan said.

"I hope not," Bill replied. "One of the reasons we want to move here is to get away from it all."

Jan murmured, "I love the crowds and the excitement of the city."

"Come to dinner tonight, and we'll try to convince you of the merits of country living."

She smiled sadly. "It's no use. If Shelley can't change me, no one can. Keep an eye on her for me."

"You sound like you're saying good-bye, Jan." The conversation scared her. Jan was more than her lover; she was her best friend.

"No, no, sweetie. But distance doesn't always make the heart grow fonder. Sometimes it works the other way."

"Who's the young man?" Bill asked. Joe was jogging toward the dock in his swimsuit with Hugo on his heels.

"My son, Joe. I think he was out all night. Probably just got back." She felt as relieved as she had when he came home safely from a late night during high school.

Joe and Hugo loped the length of the pier and dove off the end. One step ahead of the dog, Joe came up sputtering while Hugo swam in circles looking for him.

"Never could keep that animal out of the water," Bill said

"Isn't he a great dog? He always smells, though, the wet dog syndrome." She was glad to have him. Come fall, when everyone was gone, he would be her companion.

As if Jan was reading her mind, she asked, "Are you coming home for the winter months?"

"I don't know. There'll be something that needs doing here. And what about Hugo?"

"He could stay with Fred."

"Or us," Ted said.

* * * * *

Before Jan left for Milwaukee, Shelley asked her to put together an annual budget for her. "I need to know how much I have to live on." She gave Jan the expense and income books for the past year and a half.

It was five-thirty. "Don't leave yet, Jan," she said. "Stay for dinner."

"I can't, sweetie. I left too many things undone. I'll be back in two weeks on Friday. The time will fly."

The BMW purred down the driveway engulfed in a cloud of sand, absorbing the bumps and cushioning its passenger.

Part II

VII

Emily studied herself in the mirror first with and
then without her glasses. Her mother always said she
was vain. But she only needed glasses for reading.
And besides, there was nothing wrong with a little
vanity, with wanting to look attractive. But why did
she care if Shelley saw her in glasses? Shelley
probably wore them to read too.

She clattered down the stairs. "You know I'm
going out tonight."

"I know." Her mother had got skinnier in the
weeks since her father's death. Her clothes hung on

her shoulders, loose and baggy. Her hair was gray and frizzy, and there were pouches under her eyes.

Emily said nothing about her mother's appearance, knowing it would draw a wail of self-pity. Her mother had taken her father's death as a personal affront. "He died before we could enjoy retirement," was May Hodson's complaint, as if Emily's father had planned to die a few months after he found out he was riddled with cancer.

"Can you drop these books in the box at the library?" Her mother handed her a bagful of romance novels. She devoured them, yet they only seemed to make her sadder.

"Life is too short, Emily," she used to say. "I wish you liked men."

"I do like men," Emily would retort. "I just don't want to marry one."

She no longer tried to shield her mother from the facts of her life. Emily's lone sibling, a sister, had been killed in a plane accident on her honeymoon. Her parents' hopes for grandchildren had fallen on her. Only after Emily had turned forty two years ago had her mother stopped pointing out that her biological clock was ticking toward menopause.

"Anything else you want or need?"

"Where are you going now?" her mother asked.

"To have dinner with friends at Pine Shores Resort on Arrowhead Lake."

"Scott Smith owned that place, didn't he? People said it was a gay mecca. He dropped dead last winter. Fred Winslow found him facedown in the yard, his dog lying by his side." Emily's mother gave her a sharp look. "Well, don't crash into another tree. I don't want to lose everyone." Her voice quavered.

"I won't, Mom." She bent to give her mother a kiss on her velvety cheek and fled out the door. Walking across the wooden porch and down the steps, she was transported briefly into her youth, to this spot where she and her sister and their parents had spent summer evenings trying to escape the July heat.

Braking the Geo at the entrance to Pine Shores as Jan's BMW poked its sleek nose from between the towering red pines, she took off her glasses and put them on the dash. Getting out, she leaned on Jan's open window. "Leaving?"

"Yeah, I have to," Jan said. "Thanks for being such a help to Shelley."

"I owe you both."

"I think you've repaid your imaginary debt."

"Good. I can do it now for fun. See you when you come back."

"I'm going to make a vacation of it next time."

She parked next to Joe's Honda and closed the Geo's door with difficulty. The tree had shortened the car, twisting the door. Maybe soon she'd be able to buy another vehicle, she thought. Joe walked her way, a towel draped over his bare shoulder. Hugo left his side and lumbered toward her, his coat wet, his tongue hanging.

She held the dog at arms' length, away from her white shorts.

"He's glad to see you." Joe grinned, his teeth white against sunburned skin. "Where's Mom?"

"I don't know. If you see her, tell her I'm at Bill and Ted's, will you? Are you having dinner with us?"

"Naw. I've got a date."

"Someone from around here?"

"Yes. I him met last night." He held up a hand. "And don't be like Mom and tell me to be careful."

"I was going to say have a good time." They had never discussed why he should be careful.

"Mom still worries."

"So does mine. She's afraid I'll die and leave her alone." She spoke lightly.

He slapped at a mosquito. "Gotta get some clothes on. I'll talk to you later."

On her way to Bill and Ted's cabin she detoured to the dock. All day she had forced herself to stay away, because she knew Jan's visit would be short and she didn't want to be in the way.

Bill came out on the pier and stood next to her. "Pretty, huh?" The sun blazed an unbroken trail across the water, quiet now that it was after five.

"Mmm. Peaceful." Did Shelley know how lucky she was to own this piece of property? Its worth in dollars was far beyond the average person's means. She took a sip of the drink he handed her and choked.

"Too strong?"

"Nope. I need this."

"What's going on?"

"Do you have a mother?"

"Not anymore. She was a gem, though. Thought Ted and I were the cutest couple. Ted's mother was a dragon. She breathed fire. But she's not with us anymore either, thank God. What's yours like?"

"She's mad at my father for dying. I think she's angry with her life. She probably wishes unconsciously that I was the one who died instead of my sister."

"She's lucky to have you," he said, sitting cross-legged on the pier. "When and how did your sister die?"

"In a plane crash twenty years ago. She'd just married." She still felt the shock of despair as if she'd lost a part of herself, a hand or a foot. "Did you find a place to buy?"

"We have different ideas about where and what. Ted starts work September first."

"Shelley wasn't at the house."

"She's in the cabin with Ted. She seems a little down in the chops."

"If I were Jan, I wouldn't be leaving. I'd have moved here with Shelley."

"Me too, but we're not Jan. Wish you were?"

"I'd love to live here."

"How's the job?"

"Being a loan officer is not terribly exciting."

He stretched out and put his hands behind his head. "That's how I felt about being an attorney. So much tedium."

"John Grisham tells it differently."

"Fiction. Just look at that baby-blue sky. Do you think you'll stick around?"

"Oh, yeah. I'm not going anywhere. I can't afford to."

"And you just got back. Right?" He sat up and met her gaze.

She looked away. For the life of her, she couldn't think of her ex-lover without a mixture of anger and sadness. A squirt of adrenaline accompanied by tears. She hoped Barbara would someday get her just deserts, but she doubted that would happen.

"I better go help Ted," Bill said. "He'll be pissed if I don't."

"I'd be too." She brushed off her seat.

Shelley was sitting on a kitchen chair while Ted, dressed in shorts and a full apron, chopped vegetables.

"Watching the lake move?" she asked.

"Yep," Bill said. "What can I do, Teddy?"

"Make a salad."

"I offered. That apparently is your job," Shelley said. "I was telling Ted that if all my renters buy a second home or move here, I'll go out of business."

"But we want to live here year-round," Bill said.

"I know." Shelley slumped, her body settling into itself. "Hi, Emily."

Driving slowly home along a winding road through the clear night, Emily watched the roadside for deer. She knew she'd had too much to drink and couldn't risk an accident. Shelley had offered her the couch as a bed. Had it been the weekend, she might have taken her up on it.

Chicory Falls glowed in the distance, its lights rising over the surrounding acres of pine plantations and small lakes, the fields of cucumbers and corn. Named after the tall, willowy, blue wildflower found in the ditches and grassy fields in summer and fall, the village had never become a tourist trap like so many Wisconsin towns located near water. Instead, it boasted one grocery, a combined gas station and sports store, a hardware store, a building center, and numerous bars. The Chicory River flowed through the town and spilled over the dam that created the millpond.

The nearest movie theater was seventeen miles away, the closest clothing mall an hour distant. A night of entertainment for most people meant frequenting a tavern. As a teenager, she and her friends had spent their nighttime hours in the nearest beer bar or partying on DNR land or in one of the county parks that featured a beach. Now, her evening hours were spent either reading or driving the winding roads with her windows rolled down and the radio on.

She pulled into the driveway and crept into the house. No longer did her mother wait up for her return. A streetlight illuminated the stairs to the second floor. She took a couple of aspirin before climbing into bed. A gentle breeze fanned her. A branch of the sugar maple she had helped her father plant when she was five scratched at her screen, lulling her into dreamless sleep.

Someone was screeching at her. Barbara? Opening her eyes, she saw blue sky between the black maple branches and green leaves. Her mother was calling from the bottom of the stairs. A voice spoke softly from the radio on the bedside table: *Morning Edition.*

In the kitchen she drank a cup of coffee and toasted a piece of bread, while her mother puttered around the room.

"A late evening? Too much to drink?" Her mother wore shorts and a tank top. People said that Emily looked like her.

"Both," she admitted, suddenly seeing the resemblance. It was in the eyes and the bones now visible in her mother's thin face. "These people are fun."

Her mother looked at her with tired eyes. "Rumor has it that it's still a gay haven. Except for Fred Winslow working there, I'd believe it."

She nearly laughed. "Would that be so terrible? Got to go."

It wasn't that she hated working for the bank. She was grateful to have the job, but perhaps she needed a career change. Carrying a cup of coffee into her office, she studied the messages from yesterday.

Bill Hailey was waiting to see her.

He stood in her doorway, a big grin on his face. "Surprise."

"Come in. Sit down." She closed the door behind him.

"I knew you worked at the bank; I just didn't know in what department."

She sighed. Why was it people assumed she would be a teller? "Thanks again for last night."

He crossed his legs casually. Most people who came to her for money showed signs of tension.

"What can I do for you?" she asked.

"I want to buy and restore the old mill."

Her heart sank. The old mill was falling down. "I thought you were looking for a place on one of the lakes."

"It is on water. Right by the dam, the millpond on one side, the trout stream on the other."

"How much money do you need?" She hated it when friends asked her to process a loan, knowing sometimes she had to turn them down.

"It might qualify as an historic site."

"You didn't say anything about this last night."

"I want the place. Ted doesn't. Location is every-thing in business, don't you think?"

She had to agree.

After work, she met Bill and the Realtor at the old mill. The building was empty and dusty. Boards creaked under their feet. Huge windows, fragile with age, allowed them to look out at the millpond and stream rocketing over the dam. An open stairway led to the second floor and more space, more windows. There were few inner walls. She was enchanted with the possibilities, yet she knew that the old mill had failed twice as a business site in the past ten years. She told him.

"Ah, but I wasn't running it. I don't have to live off the proceeds, either. It only has to pay off the loan and buy more inventory."

The Realtor surreptitiously glanced at her watch.

"Come in tomorrow and fill out the paperwork. I'll see what I can do." As long as he didn't ask for more than the building and grounds were worth, she should be able to give him what he wanted.

He followed her outside, and they stood on the walkway over the dam as the Realtor drove away. Keening plaintively, a host of cedar waxwings swooped over the rushing water and darted from tree to tree.

"It is a lovely spot, Bill. I just hope your business instincts are good."

"It'll be a fun change."

"Do you know antiques?"

"Oh, yes. We have a houseful. Now if I can just talk Ted into parting with some of them."

"How opposed is he to this location?"

"I'm working on him." He smiled at her. "Are you coming out to the lake today?"

"I can't." It was embarrassing to keep showing up uninvited, and even harder to stay away.

"Why not? Come for a swim after work."

She smiled. "I'll see."

VIII

On the way home, Emily took a slow detour
through the town park on the other side of the
millpond. It was nearly suppertime, and the grounds
were deserted except for two guys sitting on top of a
picnic table talking, one of whom looked like Joe.
With a jolt she recognized Joe's Honda parked behind
a Ford half-ton pickup. Roger Jablonski, two doors
down, a high-school football player, drove the truck.
She identified it by the bumper stickers. Roger's
mother, Junie, had been her best friend in high
school.

She scurried off as if guilty of spying. Glancing in the rearview mirror, she saw Joe's hair shining in the sunlight.

How old was the Jablonski boy? Junie was her age, forty-two, and Roger was her next to youngest. She'd married Walter, a football and basketball star, right out of high school. Roger and his younger brother, Richard, had helped Emily unload her belongings from the Ryder truck she had rented. Her heart hammered at her ribs.

"I guess he'd be seventeen or eighteen. Why?" her mother said when she asked as they sat down to eat.

Emily helped herself to macaroni and cheese and some early corn. "Just wondered. He's so big." And he was. His neck was in line with his ears.

She called her only close friend left in Madison, Todd Fantini. It was Todd who had given her the momentum to pack her things, who had pushed her along, filling two boxes to her one. Together they had loaded the moving truck; he had fastened her Geo to the bumper hitch and waved her off. His other friends called him Fanny, but she never had.

"How's your head, honey?" he asked. Voices rose and fell in the background.

"Fine. I wanted to tell you about this gay mecca here." She smiled at her mother's choice of words to describe Pine Shores.

"Hush, you guys," he yelled without putting his hand over the receiver.

She winced.

"Make a reservation for me, Em. We'll spend a week together."

"You do it. I'll give you the number. Don't bring anybody, though. The owner has a cute son. Be safe."

"I always am," he said cheerily. "I'm the condom king."

When she hung up, she recalled how these schemes of hers never worked her way. She'd ask Bill or Ted to talk to Joe. Just in case the Jablonski boy was underage.

After cleaning up the dishes, Emily walked down the street past the Jablonski house. Junie was sitting on the porch. She looked matronly, no longer the slim cheerleader of her youth. None of the other numerous family members was in sight.

"Come on up and sit with me, Em," Junie called.

"Your boys, Roger and Richard, helped me unload my stuff."

"I know. It was bowling night or I would have come over. Sorry about your dad."

"Thanks. How's it with you?" Over the years she'd visited Junie when she'd come home, but the visits became less frequent and shorter until they shortened into a casual, passing greeting.

"Okay. You came back to be with your mom?" Junie asked.

"Yeah."

"I always thought you were smart, getting out." Junie's legs rolled out from the hems of her polyester shorts.

"Did you?" She looked sideways at her old friend. "I thought you were happy here."

"I'm happy enough, I guess. Walt is the county sheriff. I work part-time at the grocery store. Keeps me busy now that all but Roger and Richard are gone." She flecked a piece of lint off her polo shirt. "Where were you going?"

"Just walking. Want to come with me?"

"Thanks, but I'm expecting Walter home any minute. Stop by more often."

Maybe they'd have something in common now. "Sure."

She continued toward the short downtown, all of two blocks. Only the bars were open, and she went into the newest one, built next to a bait store on the shores of the millpond. The dimly lit interior swirled with cigarette smoke, mixed with the odors of beer and liquor. She gagged on the smell. It always surprised her, how many people still smoked.

Climbing on a stool, she ordered a beer on draft.

"I'll buy that," the man next to her said, swinging toward her.

She started to decline and recognized him. "Ted! What are you doing here?"

Lifting bushy brows, he said, "I could ask the same."

"I didn't know what to do with myself." It was true.

"You could have gone to the lake." Slugging back his drink, he ordered another.

"I can't go there all the time." As if she had nothing else to do. It was embarrassing.

"Sure, you can. We like having you around. So does Shelley."

"You're not there," she said. "What are you doing here without Bill?"

"Oh, I think you know the answer. We had a huge argument. I want a quiet spot on a lake; he wants this rundown building on a busy road through town."

"It's a good location for business," she pointed out.

"I know." His shoulders sloped, and he cradled his drink. "It's just that I was looking forward to a secluded place." He jerked his head toward a door in back. "Want to sit on the porch over the millpond? Get out of the smoke and smell?"

A little breeze ruffled the small body of water. The sun hung low, its light spliced by cottonwoods. She took a deep breath and smelled sweet clover. No one else was on the narrow porch.

"Is that the village park on the other side?" Ted asked.

"Uh huh." Joe's Honda was still parked in front of the Ford truck. Then she saw the two young men emerge from the woods and walk to the pond's edge.

"Looks like Joe," Ted said.

"It is Joe. He's with the Jablonski boy, who's still in high school."

"Uh-oh," Ted tsked.

"Maybe you should talk to him."

"Okay." He gave her a wry smile. "Ah, young flesh, firm muscles. I envy them."

"They'd crucify him around here. Believe me, I know. It's not a broad-minded community."

"Want another beer?" he asked.

"I'll get the next round."

"And what will Chicory Falls make of Bill and me? We'll be right under their noses."

"Maybe you shouldn't live at the mill."

The following day Bill filled out the loan request papers at the bank. "We're looking for a place on a lake again, a modest one."

Her head was thick with beer and cigarette fumes from last night. "Probably a good idea."

"I haven't compromised myself in years."

"Here maybe it's better to be discreet." She played with a paper clip on her desk. He seemed tired, older.

Leaning forward, his hands dangling loosely between his legs, he looked at her with muddied eyes. "I may put out a shingle at the mill. Do wills, powers of attorney, stuff like that."

"Sounds good," she said.

"Come on out tonight," he urged. "At least for a swim."

"Maybe after I mow the lawn."

Parking next to Ted's Saab that evening, Emily peeled off the shorts and T-shirt that covered her swimsuit.

"You want to go out to eat with us?" Ted asked.

"I grabbed a bite at home."

Bill dove off the end of the dock and came up treading water.

She glanced quickly around.

"Shelley's cruising in her bass boat." Bill grinned.

Launching herself into the air, she sliced the water neatly and surfaced near him. Not to be out-done, Ted joined them with a huge splash.

"Such style," Bill said dryly.

"When did she put the boat in?" she asked as

they floated on their backs in a semicircle, the water soft against her skin.

"Fred did, this afternoon." Ted spit a long stream. "She and Hugo have been in it ever since. She took us for a ride. She'll probably take you out now that you're here."

She grunted noncommittally, knowing she should be home, putting some distance between herself and Shelley. Instead, here she was again, unable to stay away. "Have you seen Joe?"

"Nope," Ted said, spreading his arms wide for buoyancy.

They climbed onto the dock and sat wrapped in towels while Shelley's bass boat idled toward them. Hugo stood in the bow, ears sticking out and tongue lolling. He wagged his tail and licked at their hands when they reached for the craft.

"Want to go for a ride, Emily?" Shelley asked.

"Let me get dressed first." She was back in minutes, having pulled a sweatshirt and shorts over her still wet suit.

Shelley slowly cruised the shoreline. Hugo was again up front. Emily had taken the seat behind him. Neither woman attempted conversation. The sun hung blood-red over the trees in the west, staining the clouds purple and pink and the water crimson. Steering close to the center of the lake, Shelley cut the motor.

"Do you like to fish?" Emily asked. It might be something they could do together.

"I don't know. I never have. Do you?"

"I fished when I was a kid." Her dad had taken her. She had relished having him to herself.

"You can teach me. Now that I have a fishing boat I should use it, don't you think? How about tomorrow after supper?"

"If you have time." Emily failed to note the warm rush of pleasure.

"I'll make time. Maybe I can catch enough fish to feed me through the winter." Shelley laughed, a throaty sound. "I could take up hunting too. Venison for variety, and ducks and geese. Do you hunt?" Her face was rosy, her thick hair tousled, and she squinted into the sun.

"No. Is business that bad?"

"I'm kidding, is all. It could always be worse. The well could go bad or the septic system."

"Can't Jan help you out? If need be, that is."

"No. I'll get a part-time job before I ask for money from anyone." Shelley's eyes bored into her. "There's nothing to distract us here. Talk to me."

The dog had curled up in the prow. His eyes shifted from one to the other.

Emily looked away. "What do you want to know?"

"Why you aren't with someone, for one." Shelley grinned, perhaps to remove the sting. "Am I being too nosy?"

"I don't like talking about myself." She swallowed to open her throat.

"Fair enough," Shelley said. "I'll talk. When I complain about the resort, it's not because it's a burden or anything, but because I'm afraid I won't be able to make a go of it. I love it here. I feel like I just woke up from a directionless sleep."

"I'm glad for you. Actually, I wish I were in your shoes. I'm jealous." She was, she realized.

"You have a profession. You can live anywhere. I never finished college."

"So? I'll never have enough money to buy a place like Pine Shores." And now she sounded bitter.

"It's a lot of work. You know that firsthand," Shelley said and then changed the subject. "What were you doing that evening you hit the tree? What brought you our way?"

The boat drifted toward the south side of the lake as the sun dropped behind the trees. A kingfisher chattered, flashing toward shore. A nearly half-full moon floated high in the windless sky. Shelley switched on the boat lights.

"I was driving around. There's not much else to do around here. Kind of strange that I happened upon you and Jan and Ted and Bill, isn't it?"

Shelley grinned, her teeth glimmering briefly. "Fortunate, I'd say."

She began talking quietly then. "I came home not only because my dad died and my mother needed me, but because I didn't have much choice. An attorney told me if I'd been married, I would have got half of everything. As it was, I got nothing. I'm broke." A deep sigh crawled up her throat. "She made a fool of me. That's why I don't talk about it."

"She took the money and ran?"

"She emptied the bank account and maxed out my credit card." Emily wouldn't easily be coaxed into trust again.

"Jan and I have different accounts."

"You're smart."

Dusk settled over them. Bats soared and dipped, the swallows of the night. One by one, stars popped out in the sky. Hugo had fallen asleep. She heard his slight snore.

Shelley said, "No, I'm not. I was like this boat, drifting from one place to another."

"Now you've got the resort, and Jan."

"She won't live here." Shelley looked around as if suddenly noticing it was nighttime. "Maybe we better go in."

They docked in the dark, tying the craft to the side of the pier nearest the boat ramp. Flames leaping in the outdoor fireplace threw shadowy light on those gathered around. Ted and Bill's cabin was dark, the Saab gone. Hugo stayed with the guests at the fire as Emily and Shelley said hello and made their way toward the house.

"I should go home," Emily said.

"Tonight you must stay for supper. I hate eating alone." Shelley turned on lights and poked her head into the fridge. "Want a grilled cheese sandwich?"

What she wanted was to end this tug-of-war. "I like it here too much."

"And I like having you here," Shelley replied. "Tomorrow we fish."

IX

It used to be that you could count on July being hot. This year they'd had to wait till August to feel summer as Emily remembered it. Eighties, even nineties, were not too hot for her.

She was sweating in her dress slacks and tailored blouse, walking home from work. It was August tenth, and Todd had reservations for this second week in the month. Shelley had called him with a cancellation. He was taking cabin seven and was probably already there, but Emily worked every other Saturday morning.

Jan's vacation began this week too, so Shelley would have had help this morning during the rush to ready cabins. It was presumptuous, Emily told herself, to feel responsible for Saturday mornings at the resort. She had her own obligations, work being foremost, followed by a responsibility toward her mother.

The days were shortening almost imperceptibly as the sun dipped farther toward the southern hemisphere. Emily found herself caught in a pattern of work, home, resort, a triangle in which the resort was the biggest magnet. She resented every lost minute of daylight.

Since Shelley launched her boat, they had used it to bag panfish — blue gills, perch, and crappies — and to cast for bass. She had shown Shelley how to fillet fish, and Shelley put the larger panfish in her freezer. The smaller fish and the bass she returned to the lake, as Emily did.

She waved to Roger Jablonski as he mowed his lawn. She hadn't seen him with Joe since that day she'd come across them in the park. She hoped that had been a one-time meeting, but Joe was nearly always gone when she and Shelley docked the boat around dark. Continuing toward her own house, she saw her mother kneeling in one of the flower beds, weeding.

"Let me change clothes. I'll do that," she called, wondering how many of her actions were dictated by guilt, because what she really wanted to do was pack a few clothes and get out of town.

Her mother, who looked tidier these days, rested

her fanny on her heels and wiped her forehead with her arm. "I like doing this. You go."

Overjoyed, she galloped up the stairway to her room, changed into shorts and T-shirt, threw her swimsuit, a pair of sweats, sweatshirt, and some clean underwear into the small bag along with her toothbrush and shampoo. Downstairs she passed through the living room with its worn furniture and faded rugs, into the formal dining room they no longer used, ending up in the pale yellow kitchen. The windows were large, letting in sunshine and fresh air. Vases of roses and whatever else was blooming were found in every room, their fragrance permeating the house.

Greedily swallowing a glass of well water, something she'd sorely missed while in Madison, she grabbed a banana and an apple and went through the mudroom and out the back door to say good-bye to her mother and get her car out of the old garage.

Parking next to Todd's car at cabin seven, she found him sunning on the dock.

Shading his eyes with one hand, he craned his neck up at her. "What a fabulous place, Em."

Saved from being handsome by his ears, which stuck out like Hugo's in a breeze, he was only beginning to go to seed at forty. It had been a traumatic birthday for him. He'd told her it was getting harder to work out three times a week — too boring, he'd said. His square face, set on a thick neck, was topped by dense, dark hair that nearly hid those ears. His best features were his eyes, a chocolatey brown, and his generous mouth.

"Did you come alone?" she asked, sitting next to him and removing her loafers. The water felt wondrously warm on her feet.

"Oh, yes. Haven't met the golden boy yet, only Shelley and Jan. How do you figure into all this?"

She shrugged with casual indifference. "They helped me when I ran into that tree. I help them in return. This is where it's at. There are no gay bars or clubs."

His eyes were slits. "I see. It's here or nowhere." He rolled to his belly, his head resting on his arms. "Why did you want me to come?"

"To see you, of course."

"I know you, Em. You've got something up the proverbial sleeve. For some reason you want me to woo this young man. What's his name?"

"Joe." She told him about Roger Jablonski. "I think he's desperate."

"Naw. He's just after chicken. But to me he's a chick himself. Maybe I'll give him the famous Fanny rush."

She laughed. "You do that. I'm going to put my suit on."

When she came back, he said, "I saw Barbara the other day. You should have dumped her years ago."

"I know. Did you ask her about the money or the charge card?"

"Yeah. I was proud of myself," Todd said. "She's such a bitch, she denied it all."

Emily could see Shelley talking agitatedly to Fred in the yard.

Todd followed her gaze. "Who is that hairy guy?"

"Fred Winslow. He's Shelley's right-hand man."

"Is he gay?" he asked.

"No. At least, I don't think so."

"Thank god."

"You're not going to be beautiful forever," she said, turning her attention back to him.

"Am I now?" He grinned, and he was.

Watching Shelley spot the Geo and look around for her, she waved her over.

"You two know each other?" Shelley asked, squinting down at Emily and Todd.

"Todd helped me escape Madison. I couldn't have done it on my own. He's one of my best friends; actually, he was my only friend at the time."

Todd sat up and wrapped his arms around his legs. "Lucky me," he said and ducked her light blow. "Just kidding."

"Sure you are," Emily replied, cuffing his golden tan again. "I'm staying over tonight with Todd. Where's Jan?"

"She went antiquing in Crystal Lake with three of our friends, who are staying in cabin two."

"On this blistering day," Emily said with disbelief.

Shelley shrugged. "Air in the car, air in the shops. Jan doesn't do well with heat."

"I love it," Emily said.

"I do too as long as I can cool off," Todd said, rolling into the water. "Excuse me, ladies." He swam toward the raft.

Shelley gave Emily a rueful smile. "It's too hot for some of our visitors, believe it or not. I bought eight fans this morning."

"I saw you talking to Fred. What's up?"

"Some of the cabins are running low on water. The pump runs all the time. We need a new well."

"How much will that cost?"

"Depends on how deep they go."

Emily looked at the lake. "I wouldn't think they'd have to go very far down."

"It depends on the underground reservoir and the soil. It's thirty-three dollars a foot. Then there's the pump and pressure tank on top of that." She shrugged. "Takes a lot of water to run this place."

"I'm sorry, Shelley."

"Me too." She wore shorts and a tank top. Emily thought she'd lost weight. "I'm glad you're here, though. Maybe we can get in some fishing."

"Does Jan like to fish?" Emily asked.

"Are you kidding? A mosquito might bite her. Besides, her friends are here." Shelley smiled fleetingly.

"They're your friends too, aren't they?" she inquired.

"They are. I guess." Sighing deeply, Shelley looked toward the raft. "I'm glad we had a cancellation."

"I saw Joe's car at the gas company when I left town. I thought he only worked till noon on Saturdays."

"Supposedly, but he's helping with repairs now, too. He's met someone, but he hasn't brought him home yet." Shelley sat down, took her shoes off, and submerged her feet. "The water's great, isn't it?"

"Some local person?"

Shelley sighed again. "I don't know. That might not be so good, huh?"

Emily glanced at her. "Why don't we introduce him to Todd. Todd lives in Madison."

Shelley snorted. "If Joe thinks I'm matchmaking, he'll have none of it."

Late afternoon Joe parked his Civic next to his

mother's Bronco, changed into swim trunks, and headed for the beach. From cabin seven's front porch Emily saw him striding toward the dock. She pointed him out to Todd as they sipped vodka and tonics.

"I don't have the energy to get back into my suit," Todd said. They were both burned to a crispy red. "Tomorrow I'll do my duty."

"You are getting old," she said. "What happened to the Fanny rush?"

"Tomorrow," he promised.

When they joined the other guests at the fire that evening, Joe was gone again.

"Have you met my son, Joe?" Shelley asked Todd.

"I'd like to. I saw him from my front porch. Emily said he's in graduate school."

"Business." Shelley nodded.

"I'm a dentist," Todd said as if giving his qualifications.

"That's how we met," Emily put in. The night was hot and damp, and she was thankful to be outside where a stray breeze might cool her.

Hugo lingered near the fire, looking for the occasional marshmallow, in spite of the heat.

Flanked by the three women, Jan sat away from the flames. "God, it's hot," she said.

"You can always go for a swim." Shelley's voice sharpened.

"Come with me and I will," Jan replied.

Shelley smiled, her face illuminated briefly by the leaping flames. "Okay."

Before going to bed, Todd and Emily waded into the lake.

A whippoorwill called repetitively from the other side. The stars, strewn across the blackness in patterns she could never identify, disoriented her so that she nearly lost her balance. At night the inability to see the lake bottom intimidated her. If either she or Todd went under, the odds of one saving the other would be long.

Emily had never awakened here, never stepped out onto the porch as the lake water evaporated into shreds of ghostly fog that hovered above the surface until the touch of sun dispelled them. As here, at home she heard the screech of blue jays, but not the gulls calling nor the cedar waxwings' high-pitched keening.

She quietly made coffee and took two cups to where Joe was sitting in a chair tilted against the shed nearest the ramp, there to catch the early morning fishermen launching their boats. They relied on the honor box for those who came before six-thirty.

Hugo got up to greet her as she handed Joe a steaming mug. She patted the dog's large head, which he pressed against her thigh.

"Thanks, Em," he said with surprise. "You're renting a cabin?" Red-eyed and bristle-faced, his blond hair stood in spiky clumps.

"I'm staying with my friend, Todd." She opened a lawn chair and sat next to him. "Do you always get up so early."

"Yeah. Mom would be out here otherwise, and it's

not every weekend that Jan visits. Besides, I like the mornings here."

She felt herself retreating at his mention of Jan, pulling in her head and limbs like a turtle. What was there here for her? But then she smelled the pines as the sun warmed them. And she heard the water lapping at the shore.

When Todd came looking for her, the sun was well up over the lake. "Hey, girl, when did you get to be such an early bird?" He wore rumpled shorts that she thought he might have slept in. His sleep-puffed face sported black grizzle liberally sprinkled with gray.

She introduced him to Joe, who ran fingers through his wild hair before shaking hands.

"What are you two doing here?" Todd asked.

Just then a truck backed a trailer carrying a boat toward them. Todd collected five dollars from the man driving, who drove the trailer into the water, unloaded the boat, and parked the truck and trailer in the small, grassy parking area.

"Oh," Todd said. "I didn't realize there were so many ways to make a buck."

"Hey, we maintain this boat ramp. Why shouldn't we charge a launching fee? They'd go to the public landing if it wasn't so crappy."

"I didn't mean anything. Why don't you sell him some worms, too?" Todd said good-naturedly.

The fisherman parked his truck and walked back. "Got a dozen minnows?"

Seeing Hugo contorting his body into joyous shapes of welcome caused Emily's heart to perform a cautious flip of its own. Shelley, barefoot and as rumpled as the rest of them, bent over the dog.

"I brought doughnuts," Shelley said, holding up the bag she carried. And while Joe caught minnows, she started coffee.

Emily took that time to hiss at Todd. "Why are you irritating Joe?"

He lifted his brows, managing to look guileless. "Just having a little fun."

"What happened to the famous Fanny rush?"

"All in due time."

X

They swigged coffee and ate doughnuts as the guests emerged from their cabins. There were three families with children, disclaiming the gay mecca reputation Emily's mother ascribed to this place. The kids gathered around the swings and slide and sandbox that marked the play area.

"I hear you're getting your MBA at Madison," Todd said.

"I was." Joe toed the sandy soil.

"I live in Madison."

"I don't think I'm going back this fall." Joe's pale mustache was dusted with sugar.

Uh-oh, Emily thought. The doughnut in her mouth turned dry and crumbly.

Shelley, who was reaching toward Joe's powdery mustache, fingers twitching, dropped that hand to her side. "What?" she asked.

"I like it here," Joe said to his mother. "They offered me full-time at the gas company."

"Oh, that's a real future," Shelley said.

"I'd be able to help you." His mouth thinned into a stubborn line.

Shelley looked annoyed. "It's not that I don't want you here, Joey, but you can come back after you get your degree."

"I've got one degree," he said stubbornly.

Todd met Emily's eyes and jerked his head toward the cabin. They slipped away unnoticed.

"What do you want me to do with this boy?" Todd asked. "Get him to go back to Madison?"

"If you can, and he's not a boy," she said. "He's twenty-four."

"And I'm forty." He looked thoughtful. "He's a kid, but smooth-skinned and fresh as a daisy."

"Don't put it that way, Todd."

"Are you in love with his mother?"

She sputtered, "No, of course not. She's with Jan."

"Oh, aren't we pure?"

"I told you, I owe them."

He gave her an annoyingly knowing look. "Denial."

* * * * *

That afternoon, when Todd was talking to Joe on the raft, Emily went searching for Shelley and Jan. She found Jan and her friends stretched out in chaise longues in the shade near the beach. At Jan's invitation she joined them.

"You live here year-round?" Mary asked. She was the friend who wasn't in a relationship, a handsome woman about Jan's age with a sharp cap of graying hair.

"I moved home from Madison at the end of May." She had no wish to explain more. Jan could fill in the gaps later.

Mary stared at her as if she were crazy. "You didn't like Madison?"

"I grew up in Chicory Falls," she said. "I like small towns." A doubtful statement when she considered it.

"It's a pretty place," said one of the other women.

"Where's Shelley?" Emily asked.

"In the house, I think," Jan said. "Fred promised to show her how to put new washers in the faucets. I suppose you heard about the well."

"Yes. I saw her talking to Fred. She told me."

"Do you expect Shelley home for the winter, Jan?" another woman asked.

Emily saw Mary look at Jan as if something important hinged on Jan's reply.

Jan returned the look. "I doubt it. She told me there's too much to do. She and Fred are going to reroof some of the other buildings. And besides, there's Hugo."

And maybe Joe, Emily thought, briefly wondering about the unspoken exchange that had passed between Jan and Mary

"It's probably beautiful when the snow flies," one of the women remarked.

"Breathtaking," she said, although what she remembered best about winter was the length and loneliness. The tiny library carried a meager selection of books, certainly none with gay or lesbian content. The video store offered even less choice. She conconsidered the resort an isolated phenomenon, surrounded as it was by a sea of conservative and bigoted heterosexuality. That the town hadn't descended on Pine Shores and demanded its closure she found even more amazing.

"What do you know about Fred?" Jan asked then.

Emily had mentioned Fred to her mother a couple of weeks ago and been told that he lived alone in a rundown house outside of town. "The one with all the junk in the yard," her mother had said.

Emily had driven past his house and witnessed the ancient Allis Chalmers tractor, the hulks of old cars perched on blocks, the rusted lawnmowers and other junk strewn across his yard on the banks of the Chicory. It would have been a pretty spot had it been cleaned up. Some of the house windows were boarded over, the steps to the sagging front porch were gone, and the only outbuilding was leaning and peeled of paint. She had wondered what he made of Shelley's guests, deciding that maybe he was enough of a misfit himself to tolerate differences in other people.

Smiling to herself, she recalled his gruff gentleness: "We'll patch, Shell. That'll get you through the summer. Come fall we'll take a closer look. Make do, that's what Scott done."

She said, "He does odd jobs and repairs small engines. My mother said he fixed her gutters last fall and tuned up her lawnmower."

When Jan and the others went inside for lunch, she declined their invitation and made her way to Todd's cabin. Pine needles slid under her aged loafers. She took them off and waded in the shallows, careful not to tread on the pencil weed. The midday sun seared overhead, unable to penetrate the greasy layers of sunblock she'd carefully applied.

Todd wasn't on the dock or the raft or the beach. Stepping onto the cabin porch, she caught the screen door before it banged shut behind her. In the tiny kitchen the rounded refrigerator hummed in greeting. She started toward it, suddenly hungry and thirsty, and froze in mid-step at the sounds coming from Todd's bedroom.

Turning, she crept out of the cabin and plunked down on the front steps. With her elbows on her knees, her chin in her hands, she considered what to do next. The food was inside, her book on her bed. She could get something to eat in town and come back, but her purse was in the cabin too. Maybe Shelley had something she could eat and read.

Shelley's tank top was wet with sweat, her face flushed and damp. She shoved thick, fallen hair off her forehead. "Come on in."

In the kitchen Emily's stomach grumbled at the smell of something toasting.

"Hungry? Want a bagel?" Shelley reached for the fridge door.

"I'd kill for one," she said, wondering at her own nerve. Todd was probably fucking Joe, yet here she was at Joe's mother's, begging for food.

Shelley spread cream cheese on the bagel and set the plate in front of her.

"I spent the morning with Jan and friends," she said as Shelley sat down across from her.

"Were they having a good time?"

"I think so."

"Good," Shelley said, her gray eyes clear.

"Why aren't you with them?"

Shelley picked up her bagel. "Jan and Mary are lovers."

Emily's heart began a hard thud. "Did Jan tell you that?"

"Not yet. She will before she leaves." Shelley looked nonplussed.

"But—"

"I don't care, Emily, not really. I just don't want to talk about it right now." Her smile showed strain.

"All right. Do you have anything I could borrow to read?"

Shelley showed her the books, and she squatted in front of the bookcase, running her fingers over the bindings. Picking one up, she took it to a chair on the porch.

"Read there if you like," Shelley suggested. "I'm washing sheets and towels and working on the accounts."

"Thanks. I think I will," she said, becoming immediately engrossed in the book, *One True Thing*.

* * * * *

When she returned home that night, not because she wanted to but because she knew that Todd would no doubt spend the night with Joe, it was dark. She parked in the garage and entered the house through the back door. A light burned over the kitchen sink.

"Is that you, Emily?" her mother asked.

"Yes, Mom."

She stopped dead in the open doorway between the dining and living rooms. A man was standing next to her mother in front of the sofa where they had apparently been sitting. Thick white hair fringed his bald head, which took nothing away from his good looks. He wore casual slacks and a polo shirt and was trimly built, unlike her father who had carried a paunch above his belt.

"You remember Matthew Ehrenberg, don't you, dear?" Her mother's steel gray hair fell in soft curls around her face, which glowed in the light cast by the floor lamp. She was dressed in cotton slacks and a brightly colored short-sleeve blouse.

Emily chided herself for somehow missing the changes so subtly wrought in her mother's appearance. Perhaps she'd been too caught up in her own life to see her mother developing a separate, satisfying one of her own. She tried to place this man in her previous life and failed.

"No, I don't."

"Well, Matthew belongs to our church. He was the choir director. And your father and I played bridge with him and his wife. Rita died a year before your father."

95

With sudden clarity she recalled Rita Ehrenberg, a handsome woman with two children of her own.

"I remember her. Tall with long, black hair." She wanted this man to go home and leave her alone with her mother, so that she could find out what was going on.

Matthew's eyes darkened. "Yes."

"I'm sorry. She was always nice to me." Inexplicably so, she thought.

"She loved children. At least, she got to see her grandchildren born before she died."

Emily didn't ask what had killed Rita Ehrenberg. He looked too grief stricken, and she was stunned by his unexpected presence.

"I'll just go upstairs," she said, carrying her bag through the living room.

"I thought you were staying for the week," her mother said.

She had been going to stay, but now that Todd was involved with Joe, although she hadn't been able to verify that, she felt like a third-wheel — as she did now.

Lying in bed, she strained to hear the murmur of voices through the register. Only four months had passed since her father's death, and her mother was already involved with another man.

There was no place she truly belonged, not even here. She had spent the evening at the outdoor fireplace with the other guests. Todd had vanished early on, and she assumed he was with Joe. Wasn't that what she wanted? It meant her plan to wean Joe away from Roger, if he had been with Roger, was succeeding. But it also left her very alone.

Shelley had thrown sharp words at Jan, who had

deflected them kindly, which confirmed for her Shelley's suspicions that Jan was having an affair with Mary. Otherwise, she thought Jan wouldn't have tolerated Shelley's caustic remarks. When Emily left, Shelley had walked with her to her car.

"Coming back tomorrow evening?" Shelley asked.

"Maybe, maybe not." She didn't want to interfere with Todd's love life.

But was there something to interfere with, she wondered now. She hadn't seen Todd and Joe together since late morning.

"Please come," Shelley had said.

The tips of the maple branches scratched at her screen. If she had believed in such a thing, she would have thought it was her father protesting the voices downstairs. What would he think of her mother taking up with another man so soon after his death?

Putting her disquieting thoughts on hold, she willed herself to sleep.

XI

The next morning she asked her mother about Matthew Ehrenberg.

"Oh, he's just a friend. He's lonely; I'm lonely."

"But you have me," she protested foolishly.

Her mother put a hand on hers. "Yes, dear, and I'm very happy for that. But you're gone nearly every night, and it's not the same."

"How long have you been seeing him?"

"He stopped by one evening in July when you were at the lake. He plays bridge; he bowls."

"Just like Daddy," she said, quickly realizing how easy it was to take the pleasure away. "I'm sorry, Mom."

Her mother was biting her lip, a preface to tears. "No one can take your dad's place, but nothing can bring him back, either."

She jumped to her feet, trying to hug her mother. "That was a stupid thing to say. Forget it, I didn't mean it." But the damage was done. She had seen the shine in her mother's eyes, a glow that she couldn't put there no matter how many nights she stayed home.

Her mother curled into herself, unyielding and inconsolable. "I won't see Matthew anymore, if you don't want me to."

"Dad wouldn't want that, and neither do I. I was jealous, I guess." Of what, she wondered.

Raising her head and looking into Emily's eyes, her mother said, "Oh, yes, he would. He was a jealous, possessive man."

Emily backed off a step, her arms falling to her sides. Wounded, as if her mother had said the same of her, she reacted with childish disbelief. "Daddy loved us."

"Sure he did, as long as we fell all over him. Otherwise, he punished us with silence. You don't remember?" A sad, crooked smile crossed her mother's face.

"You're just angry because he died on you," she said, looking out the window over the kitchen sink. The sky was thick with rain-drenched clouds. She'd have to carry an umbrella to the bank today. "I've got to go to work."

"I told Matthew I'd go out to dinner with him to-night," her mother said apologetically. "I thought you'd be at the lake."

"That's okay, Mom, I want you to see him. And you're right. I may go to the lake anyway."

Emily returned to a silent house after work, its large windows splattered with rain. She'd walked home, leaning into the warm, wet wind, using the umbrella to shelter her. There'd be no point in driving to Pine Shores today. Everyone would be inside.

She changed into shorts and a T-shirt and was reading the newspaper at the kitchen table while microwaving leftovers when the doorbell rang. Peering out the narrow windows next to the door, she saw Shelley standing on the porch and looking around the yard.

"Hi. What brings you here?" Emily opened the door wide. "Come on in."

"I didn't think you'd come to the lake in the rain." Shelley was now studying the living room. "What a lovely house. There's so much light, even on a day like today."

"I was just heating up some stuff. I could start over and make us some dinner, or we could go out," she said, so surprised to see Shelley out of her familiar setting that she couldn't quite grasp the implications.

"I'll eat leftovers with you, if you have enough.

Jan and the others went out to dinner. I declined."
Shelley's smile wavered and vanished.

"Let's go peek in the fridge. See what there is."
She led the way to the kitchen. "Mom's gone out to
eat tonight, too. She has a man friend. I came home
last night and found him here with her." She was
half turning to look at Shelley. "I was so startled I
said all the wrong things."

"I did that, too. My parents split ten years before
they died in a car crash together. I've always
wondered if they weren't reconciling when they were
killed. I'll never know, but I wasn't kind about their
divorce. Joey's just a chip off the old block, I guess.
He took my leaving his father very personally."

The kitchen was a warm, buttery yellow under
the overhead lights. "Would you like something to
drink?"

Shelley sat at the table and smiled at her. "What
have you got?"

"Wine. Merlot or cabernet or chardonnay. You
name it."

"Merlot, please." Shelley's gray eyes were streaked
with red. "There's something about you that makes
me talk."

"Is that good or bad?" Emily asked, pulling the
cork and pouring the wine, deciding it could breathe
in their glasses.

"Good. It eases the mind to talk about things.
Don't you think?" Shelley's smile was measuring.

Emily couldn't read her. "You look tired," she said
as they raised the wine and drank.

"I am. Jan told me last night. I knew she would.

She's always been unflinching in her honesty and her sense of fair play."

"Cheating on you doesn't qualify as fair play." She stood rooted to the floor, feeling her way through the conversation.

"Maybe not, but I wouldn't have been so honest. I would have worried about hurting her feelings." Shelley sighed. "Cheating isn't something you can hide behind a white lie." She looked toward the window. "Today was long and dreary. I spent it avoiding Jan and Mary. Tomorrow they're leaving. The other two asked if it would be all right for them to stay."

"Is it?" She hadn't moved.

"Oh, yes. I can't afford to lose any rent." Shelley looked briefly worried. The half smile that followed reminded Emily of her mother's that morning when she had been talking about her dad.

Expelling her breath in a rush, she said, "Well, I'm sorry," and thought she sounded like a broken record. Sorry about the well, sorry about the roof, sorry about Jan.

"We were good friends. I loved her mind, her commitment to her beliefs. She was comforting and never boring," Shelley said as if talking about someone dead. "I think I knew it would end if I moved here. Distance doesn't make the heart grow fonder. It just provides space for someone else to move into."

Emily opened the refrigerator and looked inside at the nearly empty shelves. "Oh, hell," she said. "Let's go someplace Jan would never think to go and get something to eat."

She chose the bar where she and Ted had spent the evening drinking a few weeks ago. "We'll sit on the back porch. There's an overhang, and no one's ever out there," she said, heading toward the back door as they both choked on the smoke.

Outside, they cleared their lungs with the warm, damp air. Rain peppered the millpond. An occasional frog croaked and a lone muskrat swam toward the far shore. Sitting on stools at the high tables, they ordered drinks, clam chowder, hamburgers, and fries.

"Bill and Ted are coming back two weeks Saturday. For good, I think," Shelley said.

"Bill needs to be here to supervise work on the old mill," Emily answered.

They were distracted momentarily when their drinks arrived. Then she looked across the millpond and saw Joe's Honda and Roger's truck. *Fuck, fuck, fuck.* What a stupid asshole she was. They could have gone anywhere and she chose here. She wanted to wave her arms and warn Joe. What was he doing here anyway instead of with Todd?

"That's Joe's car over there," Shelley said with surprise. "Who is that guy he's with?"

It was her turn to sigh. "Roger Jablonski. He lives down the block from me."

The young men disappeared into the woods.

"Oh, great," Shelley said. "This is just what I need. Joe taking up with a local boy. How old is this Roger?" She turned to pin Emily with her gaze.

"He's in high school. The son of my best friend from high school."

"No wonder he doesn't want to go back to graduate school." Shelley said. "Why didn't you tell me?"

"Because I don't really know if anything's going on."

"Oh, you can bet on it." Shelley wiped her face. "Just my luck."

"I thought he and Todd were hitting it off," she said.

Narrowing her eyes, Shelley scrutinized her. "That's why you wanted Joe to meet Todd, isn't it?"

She nodded and bit her tongue to keep from saying she was sorry again.

Before Shelley left for the resort, she extracted a promise from Emily that she'd come to the lake the following night. "I don't care if it's pouring. Less bother from the guests that way. I'll cook."

Emily's mother was not yet home. It seemed strange to wait up for her. She sat on the porch, the house lit behind her, listening to the rain in the windless night.

Having pushed her mother's words away, saving them to examine when she was alone, she reluctantly began to ascribe them to her father. Possessive and jealous, her mother had said. And Emily remembered his ominous, unexplained silences, his sitting sullenly for hours, watching TV. She and her sister had walked on tiptoes, careful not to say or do anything to trigger his disapproval.

Yet she hadn't seen her father as a controlling man. She had instead assumed that he was only looking out for her best interests when he refused to let her spend the night at her friends' houses. She hadn't cared that he wouldn't let her date until she was seventeen. She had, however, minded his early curfew when she'd been with her girlfriends.

She didn't want to be sitting on the front porch when her mother returned from her date as he had waited for her years earlier. Going inside, she climbed the stairs to her room.

In bed she opened Anna Quindlen's book and immersed herself in it. The steady patter falling through the leaves of the maple took its toll. She fell asleep with her glasses on, the book fallen on her chest, and awakened to the sound of her mother's feet on the steps. Looking at the clock, she saw it was nearing midnight. Putting the book on the end table along with her glasses, she turned out the light and slid under the sheet.

XII

Before she left for Shelley's the following night, she stopped at home to change clothes and look in on her mother, whom she'd talked to earlier in the day. She found a note taped to the bathroom mirror.

Gone to Matthew's for dinner. Don't worry. The grandchildren will chaperone. Love —

Of course, her mother hadn't meant it when she said she'd give up Matthew. It had no doubt been a ploy, one that she herself had used countless times to get someone's reluctant approval. Her mother had always wanted grandchildren. They came with Matthew, a package. She could almost hear them running through the house, destroying the quiet.

Momentary sadness seized her as she thought of the potential nieces and nephews who had died with her sister. She and Ellen had buried their sibling rivalry for good in their late teens, becoming at last close friends. She had been the younger, traipsing after Ellen and her friends as a child. Together they had skirted their father's inexplicable silences by retreating to one of their bedrooms, where they played together without their usual quarreling. Ellen's death had cut something vital out of Emily.

She dealt with despair as she always had, by pushing it away. She never allowed anyone too close, fearful that she might have to mourn another loss. Intimacy was not for her. Maybe that's why Barbara took the money, knowing her leaving would otherwise go virtually unnoticed. Emily's father's death, although it had taken her by surprise, was in every other respect unreal to her. She was unable to absorb it, to experience any deep sorrow. He was gone, vanished. She often thought and talked about him as if he were in the other room. And she knew from experience that this way he would fade bit by bit into a manageable memory.

Shaking away the funk closing around her, she wrote a note and taped it under her mother's. Maybe this would be their new mode of communication.

Gone to the lake. How about a dinner date tomorrow? You and me. Love —

Along the roadsides, bright blue chicory nodded in the hot wind under a blistering sun. Yesterday's rain had greened up the leaves and grass, brightened the flowers, cleansed the landscape. Clusters of day lilies bloomed in the ditches.

Shelley threw open the screen door to her. "Fred and I just finished cleaning out gutters. I think we might tear them off this fall before they rip out themselves. Who needs gutters in this sandy soil?" She paused and smiled. "I'm making excuses for having barely started dinner."

"We can eat after dark, for all I care." She'd been hoping for a swim and wanted to question Todd. "I brought my suit. It's so hot."

"Good. I want to swim too." A smudge of dirt streaked Shelley's forehead.

Emily smiled, glad to be there.

The lake enclosed her in a lukewarm caress. She floated on her back, spouting water at Todd who sat on the dock, dark-skinned and grinning.

"So, what's going on anyway?" she asked.

He dodged the question. "Where were you last night?"

"It was raining, and Shelley showed up on my doorstep. We saw Joe with Roger in the village park."

"I know. I waited dinner for you till seven when I gave up and ate it all. Steaks on the grill."

"What do you mean you know?" She had to extract the information before Shelley, who'd been on the phone with a reservation when she left, showed up.

"Joe was telling Roger he couldn't see him anymore." His teeth gleamed in the sunlight. "I don't know why I'm telling you, who had no faith in the famous Fanny rush."

"Is he going back to graduate school then?"

"That I don't know and can't guarantee."

"Thanks, Todd."

Todd shrugged. "He's a sweetheart. We're going out to eat tonight. Want to join us?"

"Shelley invited me for dinner."

"Aha," he said, his grin widening. "I knew it."

"You don't know anything, and here she comes, so hush." She kicked away from the dock, enormously pleased with herself that her scheming hadn't backfired. Yet.

Wings fluttered from the wetlands, startling her, as several young mallards took flight. The heron squawked and flapped into the air. Six turtles, who'd scrambled onto a log to sun, splashed into the water. She'd set off a general exodus.

Beating down with a glittering intensity, the sun covered the water with a sheen of gold that hurt the eyes. Yet she could hardly take her gaze from its surface as she and Shelley sat on the raft. It was after seven before they headed toward the house.

"What can I do to help?" she asked when they were dressed again and in the kitchen.

"Set the table on the porch, and don't expect too much. Jan was the cook."

Shelley had made enchiladas and Spanish rice with a salad on the side. They ate in silence while the last of the day's light blazed across sky and water, fading into night. The flames from the fireplace outside threw shadows over the surrounding guests, whose voices could be heard but not understood.

"What did Todd have to say about Joe?" Shelley asked, looking at her over the glow of the candlelight between them.

"When we saw Joe at the park, he was saying good-bye to Roger."

"I hope that's right." The hollows of Shelley's eyes were unreadable.

"The food's wonderful."

After washing the dishes and putting away the leftovers, they returned to the porch. Although Shelley blew out the candle, enfolding them in darkness, moths continued to batter their wings against the screens.

"Did Jan leave?" Emily asked.

"Yes. Joe, who was always very fond of her, refused to say good-bye." Shelley let out a fluttering sound, not unlike the moths "So, how was your day?"

She mentioned the brief message her mother had left on the mirror. "I suppose the grandchildren will soon be hanging around the house. I had to leave my mother a note asking for a dinner date tomorrow night. The last time I saw her was yesterday morning."

She felt Shelley's gaze on her. "You can always move in with me."

Her face flushed, making her grateful for the night. "Oh, sure."

"Why not? Then I wouldn't have to beg you to come out."

Was she really serious? "Because I couldn't —"

"Could you if we were involved?" Shelley asked.

Her breath stopped, and she forced it out. "What do you mean, *involved*?"

"I'll show you." Shelley stood and took her hand, pulling her to her feet.

"Wait. You're — I'm not —" But a flood of desire made lies of her inarticulate protests.

Shelley's low, throaty laugh only caused the dampness to spread, and she stumbled mutely in her wake.

"Look, I never meant —" she said, staring at the bed where Shelley and Jan had slept.

"I did," Shelley told her. "You know when I think I knew this would happen? When you started cleaning cabins with me. And I'm not on the rebound or whatever you were going to say. We're the only two lesbians here year-round that I know of, and I find you very attractive." Shelley shrugged.

So, this was convenient? It didn't feel that way. Her blood rocketed through her veins and arteries, and she wondered if she was having a panic attack.

"Well?" Shelley raised one eyebrow.

She'd been to bed with more women than she cared to remember, and she'd never reacted like this. In a futile attempt to tame her reflexes, she forced herself to take a deep breath. The lights were out, thank god, so that Shelley couldn't see her so out of control. "I don't know if I can do this."

"Then let's just lie down together a while. That's always a nice preface."

Lying down quickly clarified matters for her.

"Relax," Shelley said, holding her close. "You're breathing like a race horse."

She choked back a laugh. "I don't know what's wrong with me."

"I think I caught you by surprise. Have you got enough air for a kiss?"

"I don't know. I didn't expect to lose it."

"Let's see," Shelley whispered.

It made her wonder if she'd ever felt passion till then. Maybe it was because Shelley, though no bigger than herself, was luscious. Unlike Barbara, who, believing that thin was healthy, had mistakenly also thought it was attractive when carried to extremes.

She momentarily wondered how Jan could have willingly given this up. One moment she fought to breathe, the next found her caught up in the ardor, no longer reluctant or shy. Shrugging out of her shorts and T-shirt when Shelley did, she pressed against her — skin on skin. Warm and sweaty and comforting. She became lost in the kissing, willingly stalled, and Shelley had to lead her to the next stage. After they climaxed, she lay speechless at their having made love at all and would have gladly started over.

Unbidden, the shyness returned. Their relationship had been altered. No longer were they just friends. When Shelley rolled away from her onto her back, she took the gesture as dismissal.

"I'd better go," she said, reaching for her shorts and T-shirt.

Shelley was leaning over the edge of the bed, retrieving her own clothes and putting them on. "When will I see you again?"

"Well, not tomorrow. I'm having dinner with my mother, that is if she wants to have dinner with me." She was babbling, sure that Shelley was sorry and not wanting to hear her say so.

They stood, facing each other with the bed between them. Shelley switched on the table lamp, her gray eyes nearly all pupils. She smiled uncertainly. "Thursday, then?"

Emily hesitated. Shelley was not suggesting she move in anymore. The sex must have changed her mind. She wanted to flee, to hide.

On the drive home she wondered that she could have been so out of touch with herself as not to have recognized her feelings for Shelley. Her face burned with shame that Shelley, having initiated lovemaking, had determined it to be a mistake, whereas she had found it intensely satisfying.

She wondered if she would ever be able to return to the resort. Even so, she wasn't sorry. She knew she would live off the night's reruns for a long time.

Part III

XIII

Shelley had avoided Chicory Falls by shopping in Crystal Lake twelve miles away these three weeks since the night in August when she'd made love to Emily. Having turned that evening over and over in her mind, chastising herself for forging ahead over Emily's protests, she'd concluded that she'd mistaken fear for excitement.

Ted and Bill had moved into the upper story of the old mill while they looked for a home. When they bought a house, Bill said, they would store antiques in their present living quarters or use it to expand the store or, better yet, she could live there during the winter months. But then she would risk running into Emily.

The summer guests were gone, the resort deserted. She'd thought during the busy months that she'd look forward to a little free time, but that was before Emily left her life and Bill and Ted moved into town. Now she dreaded the coming winter.

The day was gorgeous with the sumac turning, the bergamot and blazing star and ironweed blooming in the ditches, the sky a bright blue. At the beginning of the summer the beauty around her had been enough, but not now.

She braked, spying a bunch of sandhill cranes in the field off to the left. Putting the Bronco in park, she studied through her binoculars their huge gray bodies, long necks, red-capped heads, and stork-like legs as they pecked at the ground.

Over dinner that night Joe announced that he was returning to graduate school.

"Good," she said, hiding her immediate despair. After all, this was what she wanted for him. Her feet snubbed up against the dog lying under the table. "Get out from there, Hugo," she snapped.

"The gas company let me go, said there wasn't enough for me to do." He looked glum.

"It's not too late to get back in the master's program?" she asked.

"I don't know, but I hate to leave you here, Mom. Winter's coming."

He pushed his food around the plate, not eating.

From under his sun-bleached mop of hair, his eyes looked dully into hers.

"I'll be fine. There's always Fred."

He glanced at the dog that was crawling out from under the table. "And Hugo and Bill and Ted and Em."

"When are you leaving?"

"As soon as I'm packed." He gave her an imploring smile, his dimples deepening.

He always said she only thought he was cute because she was his mother, so she didn't say it. "I'll miss you terribly."

"Me too, Mom. I will come back." He leaned over and thumped the dog on his side. "You behave, Hugo."

Hugo lumbered to his feet and put his large head in Joe's lap, no doubt looking for a treat, unwittingly breaking the tension, making them laugh.

The last week in September, Shelley stood by with Hugo, watching as the well-drilling rig bored relentlessly into the dry ground. When she tired of the noise, she wandered away with the dog at her heels and drove the garden tractor and trailer out of the storage shed. Now that she no longer had guests, Fred only came when she needed him. He would help her close the cabins in October. Together they had reroofed the cabins that needed it, had fixed screens and painted where necessary. He'd cut down two dead oaks, which she split with the wood splitter.

She had never been so lonely. Tomorrow she planned a drive into Crystal Lake to apply for a part-time job. There had been a help-wanted bulletin at the IGA. It would give her much needed money until the estate was settled.

Later in the day she set up the bird feeders in the yard. The guests were gone along with most of the lake property owners, and the migrating birds were on the move. She intended to entice with sunflower and thistle seeds the birds that braved the winter.

When she went inside at sunset, the phone was ringing.

"Joe stopped over to say good-bye this morning," Bill said. "I've been trying to get hold of you all day. Are you all right?"

Looking outside at the red glow in the west, she wondered why sundown now created an inexplicable longing when it had stirred only appreciation earlier in the summer. "Fine," she said, but there was a quaver in her voice.

"You don't sound that way. Come on over, will you? Bring Hugo."

"All right." With night coming on, she hadn't the heart to stay alone.

She drove along the black roads toward Chicory Falls. Hugo sat tall on the passenger seat, his nose poking through the partially open window, noisily sniffing. There would be slobber all over the glass, but she didn't care. He was her only companion.

Bill ascended the open stairway with her toward the intoxicating smells of Ted's cooking. "It's been a tough day for you," he said.

And suddenly, unexpectedly, she began to cry.

"Sit." He urged her into a cranberry-colored easy

chair near one of the tall windows that overlooked the dam and lowered the blinds that covered half the glass.

As she watched Hugo snuffling around Ted's feet, her tears dried up. After all, she'd chosen to live here, knowing she'd be alone. She'd be damned if she was going to whine about it now.

"Move in here when we move out," Bill suggested as he had before. "You can work part-time for me in the antique store. I have to go on buying trips."

"But I need to make some money." She couldn't afford to exchange work for rent.

"I'll pay you, honey," Bill said as if to a child.

She smiled. "I know you will, but there's the rent."

"No, no, no." He shook his head emphatically. "You'd be watching over the place for us."

"And who would watch over the resort?" she asked.

"No one will bother it, way out there. You can go home on the weekends."

Over a dinner of mustard chicken and fried rice, they told her they had signed an offer that day for a home on nearby Goose Bay Lake.

"If you really want someone to live here, ask Emily. I'll work, though, when you want me to, when I can." She needed the money.

"Think it over, Shelley," Bill said. "Don't give me an answer yet."

"What's going on with you and Emily, anyway?" Ted asked, refilling their wine glasses with a chardonnay.

"Absolutely nothing."

"But you're friends." Bill looked puzzled.

Her tongue loosened by the wine, she tried to explain.

"Let me get this straight," Ted said. "You made a move on her, she went along with it, and you haven't seen each other since. Why?"

"I think I coerced her."

They guffawed.

"Bullshit." Bill raised his glass. "We've been wondering what happened. She probably thinks you don't want to see her, especially after all this time."

"Want to spend the night?" Ted asked.

"I didn't bring any stuff with me."

"You can wear one of our T-shirts, and we've got an extra toothbrush."

"All right," she said meekly.

They walked the dog over the dam to the park on the other side before going to bed. The rushing water drowned out all other sounds, while the clouds played hide-and-seek with the stars.

The following morning she wakened on the couch to the smell of coffee dripping. Ted, wrapped in his bathrobe and bathed in sunlight, stood looking out the window toward the stream.

She sat up and ran fingers through her hair. "Thanks for letting me stay last night, but I can't live here. I'll work for Bill when he needs me."

Bill came out from behind the screen where they slept. "You're a stubborn woman."

"I know. But I wanted to live at the resort. Yesterday overwhelmed me, is all, with Joe leaving so suddenly. The big city girl in me panics when I think of the solitude of winter, but I think that'll change."

Hugo woofed in her face.

"Got to go out, don't you?" She looked at the men. "At the lake I can just open the door. Here I have to put him on a leash." She pulled on jeans and clambered down the steps, out into the morning.

The ground was warm underfoot from yesterday's sun. She walked the dog across the bridge to the park, grateful to Bill and Ted for the haven they'd offered her last night but ready to go home.

When she'd left for Bill and Ted's last night, the well drillers had gone for the day, leaving the rig behind. When she returned home, they were at it again.

"Haven't hit a clear vein yet," one of the men shouted as she held Hugo by the collar. "We're into sludge here."

"How far down?" she yelled over the noise.

"Thirty-five feet," he hollered back, reaching out to pat Hugo.

She released the dog, who sniffed the man's crotch. What was it about dogs? She took him in hand again. "I don't understand. The lake's so close. There should be water not far down."

"There is, but the soil conditions have to be right for it to flow. You gotta have a good supply of it here. It's like a stab in the dark, hitting a clean water vein." He gestured toward the drilling rig, clanging as it brought up dirt. "We have another job to do tomorrow."

"You're going to finish this one first, aren't you? I have to have water." She could see the costs skyrocketing out of control.

"We'll keep at it," he said. "Hopefully, we won't have to abandon this one and start again."

She looked at him with horror. Perhaps he just pointed out the worse scenario to make the cost of a deep well more palatable.

The house greeted her, cool and empty. Except for the humming refrigerator and the ticking of Hugo's toenails, silence prevailed.

She supplied the drillers with coffee and the sweet rolls she had bought in town. At fifty-two feet, they brought up a fresh, plentiful supply of clear water.

After installing the pump in the casing and replacing the pressure tank with a new, larger version, they left. With one hand on Hugo's ruff, she watched their rig and pickup truck disappear into the winding, tree-lined driveway. Feeling suddenly alone, she looked around, then recalled her plan to drive to Crystal Lake and apply for a job. It would have to wait till tomorrow.

XIV

On a Saturday at the beginning of October, Emily sat with Ted on the enclosed front porch of his and Bill's new home on Goose Bay Lake. The honking of geese overrode all other sounds, including ducks, on this stopover in their migration route.

Bill appeared in the doorway. "Hi, girl. Hello, boyfriend. What's happening."

"Just watching the geese fly. What's new with you?"

"I have a proposition for Emily."

"What?" she asked, her interest piqued.

He plopped down next to Ted on the wicker couch. "I don't want you to say yes or no right away, Em. I want you to give this serious consideration."

"All right. Tell me what it is," she said, realizing Bill no longer looked nondescript to her, nor puny. If asked to describe him, she would have said he had a sensitive face and warm eyes.

"The apartment above the antique store is up for grabs. The rent is the cost of utilities. And there are the amenities, which include a water-view and a convenient location for work and shopping. You can walk anywhere in town."

"I already live in town with my mother," she said.

"That's the point," Ted said. "You told us you wanted privacy, your own place, where the boyfriend's grandchildren can't bother you."

Oh, she'd said those things all right. "I was just blowing off. Mom wouldn't understand. Besides, I haven't even met these kids yet." She had trouble envisioning Matthew as a boyfriend; he was too old.

"Think about it," Bill urged. "Don't give me an answer now. I don't want just anyone up there. You'll be doing me a favor by moving in." His eyes caught hers. "Shelley said you might be interested in the apartment."

A slow burn crawled up from her toes. She didn't want Shelley making suggestions about where she should live. "What's it to her?"

"Hey, she cares about you," Ted said.

She blew scornfully. "Sure, she does."

"Just give it some thought," Bill persisted.

"She works downstairs." She'd run into her.

126

"There's an outside staircase." Bill grabbed the binoculars. "What kind of ducks are those out there?"

"Goldeneyes," Ted said.

"Joe's gone, you know."

"I know," she said.

"She's lonely."

Ted shot a glance at Bill and added, "They had to go pretty deep to find water for the new well."

"Costly." Bill put down the glasses. "Those are goldeneyes."

"I'll think about the apartment," she said, wondering what kind of a friend she was. Never there when needed.

Back home, her mother introduced Emily to Matthew's grandchildren. Placing a hand on one little girl's head, she said, "This is Caitlyn," then moved to the next and smaller girl, "and this is Chelsea," and on to an even shorter boy, "and, last but not least, Chad."

All *C*'s, Emily thought disparagingly, until she recalled that her own and her sister's names began with *E*. She wanted to ask her mother if that had been on purpose, but she seldom spoke of Ellen to her mother. Maybe it would be safe to do so now that these three children had become something like foster grandchildren. With mock solemnity she shook their hands.

"Want to play catch?" Chad asked. "I brought my ball."

"We get to play too," Caitlyn said.

She found herself outside in the warm, golden afternoon with dust motes dancing in the sunlight, tossing a soccer ball to the kids who ducked rather than grabbed it. She wriggled out of her sweatshirt.

"Let's kick it down the yard. Okay? See the garage? That's one goal. The other is the back steps to the house." She figured it would be less boring than standing still.

After fifteen minutes of booting and chasing the ball because the kids dodged it or missed every time, she gave up.

"I'm hot. What about you three?"

"Yeah," they said.

"Let's go play cards," Caitlyn suggested.

There was no escape. She hoped that they played cards better than they did soccer. They gathered around her, all talking at once. Like chicks around a hen, she thought, brushing Chelsea's hair out of her eyes.

Sunday afternoon she set out determinedly for the Antique Mill, having spent the morning raking and piling leaves in the gutter for the county to suck up and dispose of. Burning was forbidden, banishing the smell from her childhood that she associated with fall.

Gathering her courage around herself with a deep breath, she stepped inside the old building. A bell on the screen door jingled as it closed behind her, and a sweet breeze, carrying the smell of water, swept past her. Cast iron doorstops propped open both the front and side doors. Sun filtered through the tall windows and screens, and Hugo's tail thumped the sun-baked floor as he struggled to his feet and ambled over to her.

Shelley looked up from the sales ticket she was writing, her face registering surprise. "Well, hello." She bagged the item she'd sold and handed it to the buyer, an older woman.

"Thanks. Come again."

Emily studied the merchandise with pretended care, aware that Shelley was watching her.

"Have you been here before?"

"Yes, when Bill was working. He and Ted told me about the new well. I knew that Joe left."

Shelley crossed her arms and shrugged. "Lots of water now, and Joe had to leave sometime."

"I'm sorry, Shelley."

"For what? I'm the one who should apologize."

"I haven't been much of a friend."

Shelley looked amused. "And we should talk about why."

The bell jangled again as three women walked through the door.

Emily continued her explorations, running her hands over the furniture, picking up plates and books, questions clattering unanswered in her thoughts.

When the women left, each purchasing a Christmas ornament, she asked, "Is there lots to do at the lake?" She could offer help.

"In two weeks Fred and I will close off the water to the cottages and drain their systems. Come out any time."

She smiled. "I will."

"Soon," Shelley said.

"Okay, but you're not home on the weekends anymore."

"That's true. I wonder what Bill will do for help in the summer?"

"Then you will be opening in the spring?"

"Oh, yes. The resort has to pay for itself, so I work my head off to keep it and never have much time to enjoy it. Doesn't make sense, does it?" Shelley sat on the edge of the desk.

They were talking about everything but what had set them at odds, but at least they were having a conversation again. It seemed to Emily as if they had never stopped.

"Do you like working here?"

"I love it. All the worry is Bill's." Shelley smiled brightly. "How's it going for you? Is your mother still seeing that man? Are you a surrogate aunt yet?"

She laughed. "I met the little darlings yesterday. Actually, they're nice kids. But I think I will move upstairs here." The decision had made itself, jumping out of the unexamined recesses of her mind.

Shelley's smile became determined. "Good. I'll see you more often then, won't I?"

Gravel crunched, a car door closed, and Bill came in the side door. "Did the mountain come to Mohammed, or was it the other way around?"

Bill and Ted helped Emily move in the following weekend. Her mother cried, but Emily imagined she saw relief through the tears. Now Matthew could spend the nights there as well as the days and evenings. She wouldn't be in the way, yet she wished her mother wasn't in such a hurry to replace her father.

"I'm within walking distance of home, Mom."

That evening she baked frozen pizzas in the apartment-size stove, pulled the cork from a large bottle of cabernet and invited Shelley to come upstairs after she closed the shop.

She'd hung most of her clothes in the wardrobe behind the screen that hid the sleeping area, and put the dishes and pots and pans and utensils and tableware in the cupboards and drawers under and above the counters that delineated the kitchen. Her chair, couch, desk, end table, and lamps were arranged in the remaining open living space. A few rugs brightened the wood floors.

Outside the windows, whose lower panes louvered out, the trout stream rushed by. She heard it over their voices as background music. The venetian blinds covered more than half of the eight-foot-high windows. Bill had painted the walls an off-white. During the day the apartment dazzled in the light flowing in, and now, as she switched on the lamps against the dusk, it was as if she turned on daylight.

Hugo thumped down on one of the throw rugs, banging his tail on the wood floor.

"I hate to eat and leave, but I must," Shelley said.

"Why is that?" Ted asked.

"I have to get up early tomorrow. I took a part-time job at Stop'n Shop."

"Why? Don't I pay you enough?"

"The well was expensive, and the estate isn't settled yet."

"Want a loan?"

"No," she said emphatically. "I couldn't accept. Besides, I'd have to pay you back."

When everyone left, Emily stood looking through the blinds at the trout stream falling from the lip of the dam and stumbling over the boulders at the bottom of the falls. Beyond, the millpond glinted a dull pewter, surrounded on three sides by a black wall of trees. Shadowy rectangular buildings completed the enclosure.

Life had caught her by surprise again. As usual, someone else had provided the momentum. She'd gone along with the flow. One step forward, two steps back. Eventually, she'd ended up where she began. Was that bad? Maybe this is where she wanted to be.

Turning away from the window, she closed the blinds and turned out the lights. Through the uncovered expanse of glass above the blinds, she glimpsed the sky. Stripping to her panties she crawled into her bed and studied the stars.

XV

Checking out and stocking shelves at Stop'n Shop took most of Shelley's spare energy. Standing all day made her back ache and her feet burn. In all her working years she'd never made more than fourteen thousand a year at any one job, but at least she'd had benefits. Stop'n Shop hired mostly part-time, so that they wouldn't have to pay health insurance.

On October fifteenth she and Fred drained the water from the water heaters in the rental cottages, flushed and dipped out the backs of the toilets, put antifreeze in the bowls and blew out the water lines. It was late afternoon when they finished.

"You want me to plow you out regular?" he asked before leaving. She wouldn't be seeing him much till spring.

"Please." The day was shirt-sleeve warm, making it difficult to imagine snow.

"Then sit tight till I git you out. Don't go getting yourself stuck and clogging up the road."

She nodded. His admonitions amused her. Always gruff, he became especially so when his concern for her showed through.

"By, old dog." He banged Hugo affectionately on the side before climbing into his rusted truck.

She raised one hand. The other rested on Hugo's warm coat. "How old is he?"

"Don't know. Ten years maybe."

"Take care, Fred." She buried her fingers in the dog's thick hair as he pressed against her.

The fall colors had peaked or were peaking, the red and yellow leaves vividly accented against the many evergreens. She took a few tentative steps toward the woods, and Hugo grabbed a downed branch in his jaws and raced ahead. Now, her choices were to take a walk or disappoint the dog.

Shambling through fallen leaves, she followed Hugo into the woods. The largest of the pines lay on the forest floor. The first downed tree she assumed had fallen on its own, but when she noticed another and then more, she examined their trunks. Sawdust clung to the rings that marked their years. Piles of it clustered around their stumps. Someone had cut them recently. They rested several feet inside the woods, invisible from the driveway.

The senseless taking of mature trees pained her. It felt like murder. She was stunned by the loss and pondered what to do till Hugo, barking at her feet, brought her to her senses. She would call Bill first before she called the sheriff. Somehow, a friendly presence would make the loss more bearable.

"I'll lock the store and be out as soon as possible." His voice comforted her.

She was sitting on the picnic table when the sheriff's car trailed Bill's new Suburban down the driveway. Thrilled at the prospect of another walk in the woods, Hugo led the way. All three carried flashlights, even though the sun hadn't yet dropped out of sight. It felt like a summer evening.

The sheriff said the obvious, "Someone cut them all right. If we catch whoever did it, they'll have to pay you market value for the trees. You can sell the wood for pulp, you know. That's what they were planning to do, I expect. Slither them logs out of there and sell them."

But she hadn't planned to harvest the trees. She wanted them back in the ground, alive.

"How were they going to do that without bringing in heavy equipment?" Bill asked.

"They could be in and out of here in a day, while Ms. Benson was at work."

"They'd have to know I was gone." Someone must be watching her. The thought sent shivers galloping across her skin. She looked at Hugo, stretched out on the linoleum next to her.

"We may never catch them, Ms., but I'll get out here to check at least once a day or send my deputy. Call if you know anything." He disappeared into the warm night.

135

Bill asked, "You know who the sheriff is?"

"I didn't catch his name."

"Walt Jablonski. He's Roger's father. Maybe you should move in with us for a while."

She looked at him with alarm. "Why?" Glancing at the dog, she said, "Think I should lock him in the house when I'm gone?"

His light brown eyes met hers. "Yes. Want me to stay the night?"

"No. We'll be fine."

She bolted the doors behind him.

When Hugo barked in the night, she awoke afraid and heard owls hooting back and forth, one close by.

At Stop'n Shop the next day she stocked shelves, which was good because it required little thought and she was frazzled from lack of sleep and distraction. The what-ifs crowded into her brain. What if they broke into the house and hurt the dog? What if they came back and cut down the rest of the trees? What if they broke into the storage buildings and stole the boat, the garden tractor, the snowmobile?

She eyed the clock as the hands crept across its curved surface, willing them to move more quickly to three o'clock when she could leave. Her heart hammered its angst whenever she allowed her imagination to wander.

"Is something wrong?" her supervisor asked her.

"No. Why?" she said.

"I thought you'd be done with this department by now." It was eleven A.M.

"I'll hurry," she promised.

When three o'clock finally arrived, she sped toward home. Hugo barked in welcome. She was so relieved to see him alive and the resort intact that she felt weak and inexplicably grateful.

"Come on, big boy. We'll go for a walk as soon as I change."

The dog followed her into the bedroom and lay panting on the rug in the bedroom while she put on jeans and a sweatshirt. Then he pushed through the door in front of her and, with ears flying, dashed toward the woods.

She half expected the logs to be gone, but they remained scattered like pickup sticks at the feet of the remaining pines and oaks. When she got back inside, she would call the logging company and ask if they would buy them. It seemed unfair that even if caught, the transgressors couldn't make things right. They couldn't undo their crime.

Geese honked overhead, their V formations etching lines in the sky. They never flew without announcing their presence. It took energy to honk and fly at the same time. On the edge of the woods, she watched them head for the lake, landing with wings braking and legs trailing.

She heard and saw the sheriff's department car at the same time.

A tall man with a large belly stepped out, adjusting his gun belt to align with his pants, and introduced himself. "Deputy Haines, ma'am." He extended a large hand, and hers disappeared into it.

"I was just going to call the logging company," she said.

He looked around at the buildings and grounds. "You all alone out here?"

"Except for Hugo." Hugo wagged his tail, and she stroked his head.

"Is he a good watchdog?" Haines's eyes were small in the flesh of his face.

"Well, I don't think he'd bite anyone. He's more likely to lick them to death," she said, smiling at the image.

Haines hitched up his pants. "We kind of think you might be at risk here, ma'am." He appeared uncomfortable.

"Why?" Had he heard something?

"Well, because you're so isolated."

Bill and Ted must have said something. "You know anything I don't?"

He cleared his throat. "No."

"This is my home. I need to watch out for it."

"All right, Ms. Benson. We'll keep an eye on you."

She liked him for his deference, his concern. "Call me Shelley."

Dark set in quickly this third week in October, and no matter how warm, once the sun was gone she no longer lingered outdoors. Putting a pan of water on to boil, she got out a jar of spaghetti sauce, while carrying on a running monologue with the dog.

When Hugo lifted his head off his paws and barked at the door before getting up to go to it, her heart momentarily stopped.

"Who's there?"

"Emily."

Drawing her inside, she bolted them in.

"What is it?" Emily asked, her blue-gray eyes nearly black.

"Nothing. I'm just terrified is all." She laughed nervously.

"Because somebody cut your trees down?"

"I guess." She gestured at the door. "And of whoever's out there."

"I didn't see anyone."

"Brave of you to come here after dark."

Emily looked at her strangely. "I was here after dark most of the summer."

"When the place was full of people."

"Shelley, you were certainly in more danger when you lived in Milwaukee."

"You're right. I'm spooked by the shadows, the silence and," she said, alarmed again, "by what has happened."

"Then why don't you move in with Bill and Ted?"

"Why didn't you move in with me when I asked you to?" She hadn't known she was angry about it. "You moved into Bill's apartment instead."

"You only mentioned moving in once. I thought you changed your mind."

"Oh." She felt deflated and dropped into a chair. "You never came back after that night." Staring at Emily, she tried to glue her in place. "Was it a misunderstanding?" Jan would have told her, but Emily wasn't Jan.

"I thought you wanted me to leave."

She held Emily's gaze. "Are we talking about the same thing? The night of August thirteenth?" A nervous grin crept across her face.

Emily nodded, looking ready to flee.

"When you were in such a hurry to get out of here, when you didn't call or come over, I thought I'd pushed you into doing something you didn't want to do."

"You didn't call, either," Emily said, apparently

rooted to the floor. Her freckles stood out against her skin.

"I didn't want to pressure you, and then, you know how it is. Time passed, and it became impossible to make the first move." She almost reached for Emily's hand. "But you came to see me at the shop."

"I thought I'd been a lousy friend when Joe left and Bill and Ted told me about the well being so costly."

"Stay for supper, stay the night. You can sleep in the other room if you want."

They both jumped when the pounding on the door brought Hugo to his feet, barking, but it was only Ted and Bill.

"We brought dinner." They held up a bottle of wine and a pan of lasagna. "All we need is a salad."

"You could organize and take turns coming over, so I'll never be alone," she said, her fear gone.

"Instead of all appearing at once?" Bill opened the windows to let the heat from the kitchen escape into the unseasonably warm night.

"I have this feeling that winter is going to descend on us without warning and refuse to leave," Ted said.

"Unlike him, I can't wait for the snow to fall," Bill enthused.

"I found my uncle's snowmobile suit the other day." Shelley had been looking through boxes in the attic. She had also discovered old family albums with photos of her parents and brothers and herself, pictures her uncle must have taken before becoming estranged. Perhaps she should make contact with her brothers.

"Does the snowmobile run?" Emily asked.

"Fred got it ready to use before he left," she answered.

"Here's to Fred." Bill held his glass up to toast.

"Does Fred know about the trees?" Ted asked.

Shelley shook her head. "He left just before I found them."

XVI

"I have to work tomorrow," Emily said after Ted and Bill went into the warm night.

"I know. So do I. If you don't want to stay, don't feel as if you have to. I'm not scared anymore," Shelley told her.

"Yes, you are." Emily looked away. "And I don't want to go."

"Then don't." Shelley took her hands. "I won't make you do anything you don't want to do."

"You never did," she said, gently extracting her sweaty palms.

"Look at me."

Her head snapped up at the command, but Shelley's gaze was so intense, she felt as if she were about to lose herself and broke eye contact.

"Tired?" Shelley asked with a wry smile.

"Exhausted." Uncertainty did that.

"Me too. Will you sleep with me or do you want your own room?"

"I'll sleep with you. We'll both feel safer."

The dog padded after them into the bedroom and thumped down on a braided rug.

"Do you need a nightshirt?" Shelley asked, her eyes large and luminous in the dimly lit room.

"I'll wear my undershirt. It'll do." Feeling oddly detached, she stripped and got between the cool sheets. She stared at the overhead fan. The mattress moved under Shelley's weight.

"How do you like your new place?" Shelley asked, switching off the table lamp.

"It feels strange. It's been a long time since I lived alone."

"Me too," Shelley said. "Wake me up if I snore."

She laughed. "Good night."

In the wee hours, wakened from a sound sleep by Shelley's touch, she could hardly believe she'd drifted off. She had never slept well with another person in the bed. Lying on her back, she pretended sleep as Shelley's hand roamed over her body.

But when Shelley reached beneath her undershirt, she came to life. The passion exploded inside her and manifested itself with lovemaking so aggressive and intuitive that later she would wonder at herself. She had never before allowed desire to blot out her inhibitions.

She found herself on top of Shelley, her tongue in Shelley's mouth, her fingers already exploring and penetrating.

Shelley made a low sound.

She paused. "Am I hurting you?"

"No, not at all."

The dog let out a series of yips.

"He's dreaming," Shelley said. "Take your clothes off."

Emily rolled on her back and discarded her panties and undershirt off the side of the bed while Shelley did the same. Then they pressed against each other, kissing and stroking until both were moving in a timeless rhythm.

"I've wanted to taste you for the longest time," Shelley whispered. "Can I?"

Emily froze momentarily, then realized that she wanted that, too. "Yes."

They came quickly, urgently, loudly.

Hugo barked.

After, they lay in position for a few more moments until their breathing slowed. Shelley turned around and pulled the sheet over their cooling bodies.

Struck by the intensity of the sex, Emily waited for Shelley to speak first.

Finally, Shelley did. "Nice loving. Fireworks, the whole ball of wax. How was it for you?"

"You pretty much described it."

Shelley looked at the clock. "For close to an hour I forgot where I was and what was going on. Can we start over?"

Emily laughed.

"Will you move in with me now?"

She could feel Shelley's gaze. "I just moved."

The next morning she arose at six, drank a cup of coffee with Shelley and drove home to shower and dress for work, still dazed by last night's passion. She patted Hugo good-bye and found herself parked next to the old mill, recalling none of the drive. Remembering a fellow employee who had married and for weeks after looked besotted, she at last understood the lust in his eyes. It was in hers. Throughout the day, she relived the previous night's passion, making her virtually useless at work. She wondered how Shelley felt.

The lovely, warm fall days fell under November's bitter winds and unseasonably cold temperatures. Shelley sold the fallen pines for pulp. She grew complacent when weeks passed and nothing more happened. The trees became for her a random act of vandalism.

Her lust for Emily made her uneasy. She believed in balance. She considered this longing for sex, this all-consuming passion, a weakness. They made love every night, sometimes more than once. She had never felt this way about Jan or anyone else.

Yet Emily wouldn't move in with her and shied away when asked. When Shelley worked at the antique store, she spent the night upstairs in Emily's apartment. She understood why Emily liked it there. The bright, open space, the huge windows with their views of the small millpond and the rushing Chicory River, the proximity of work and store.

She ate Thanksgiving dinner with Ted and Bill. Emily was having dinner at her mother's house. The snow started toward evening as she was leaving. She drove through the thickening white flakes to the old mill and let herself in.

Emily looked up from a book as she and Hugo came into the room. "I heard the Bronco. They're predicting six inches. You're working here tomorrow, right?"

She removed her jacket and hung it on a chair to dry. "Yep. How was your day?"

"Different. Matthew was there and his daughter and son-in-law and the kids. I like the kids. Actually, I like them all. But I would have rather been with you and Bill and Ted." Emily took off her glasses and put the book down. "Do I get a Thanksgiving hug?"

"How about a Thanksgiving fuck?" she said, grinning.

"All right. Maybe it'll help me digest."

Shelley tugged at Emily's clothes. "Take these off."

After, Shelley lay on her back, her arms around Emily, whose head rested on her shoulder. The room was never dark with the blinds only halfway up the windows. Nevertheless, the falling snow blotted out the sky. She wanted always to be this content.

Jan had been the planner, not herself. Now she wanted to sketch out her life with Emily, and Emily would have none of it.

"Are you happy, Emily?"

"As happy as I've ever been."

"Me too."

She awakened early to four inches of snow on the ground, enough to turn the landscape a blinding white. The sun was barely up, but still she squinted when she took Hugo out to do his stuff. Once they crossed the dam, she unsnapped the leash and he ran free. Blue jays screamed; blue flashed against the brilliantly white crystals. She had filled her feeders two days ago. Bill had promised to check them this morning.

After wiping Hugo's feet, she went to the bathroom to wash and warm her hands under the faucet before climbing back in bed and waking Emily, much as she had that night in October.

Emily stirred. "There's not enough time, sweetie," she murmured. "Tonight."

Here she was at forty-seven, lusting shamelessly. It made Shelley laugh. "I'll make the coffee."

Bill brought Thanksgiving dinner leftovers at noon. "I had to go to the bank. Thought you and Em might like an easy meal tonight."

"Thanks." She carried the food to the fridge upstairs.

"I filled your feeders this morning," Bill said when she reappeared. "The storage building was broken into and your snowmobile's gone. I reported it to the sheriff. I'll fix the lock after he sees it. Want to close up shop and go out with us?"

Stunned, she stared at him while she digested this unexpected information. Her heart beat against her ribs. It hurt to breathe.

He went upstairs, got her jacket, helped her into it, and led her out the door, which he locked behind them in Hugo's face.

They stood, hands in pockets, looking around the storage building.

"Anything else gone?" Haines asked.

She shook her head, looking at the tracks leading away from the building.

Haines said, "Whoever took it loaded it on a trailer in the road. Do you have the make and model number?"

She'd never be certain it was hers, even if she saw it. "Maybe somewhere in the house. My uncle bought it. It was a Ski-Doo, if that helps." She'd had visions of being so snowed in that she'd have to use the snowmobile to get to town. So much for that.

Haines left, promising to keep a closer watch on the place. Bill had brought out new hinges and another lock, and he screwed those on while she went to check the house and the other buildings. Knowing she'd have to spend her nights here, keeping watch, she turned up the heat to make the house less cold and unwelcoming.

Emily understood but was not thrilled with Shelley's unwillingness to any longer divide their nights between the resort and the old mill, especially now during the last weekend of deer hunting season.

The woods swarmed with orange jackets and hats. Sporadic shooting could be heard in town. Outside the village it was sometimes a volley. She knew the killing was necessary, that it beat a death by starvation, yet she hated seeing a sleek deer dragged out of the woods by someone unshaven and unclean. She'd feel better when the weekend was over. Here hunting was a way of life, a rite of passage for young boys.

A skim of ice covered the lake, thickening at night, thinning during a sunny day when the temperatures rose into the thirties. She went to her mother's house on Sunday afternoon, while Shelley worked at the Antique Mill.

"I can never reach you at your apartment anymore. Don't you answer the phone?" her mother asked. She looked years younger than she had last April. Her hair, although grayer, was permed and styled. Everything about her vibrated with life — her snapping blue eyes, her quick gestures, her straight posture.

"I've been spending nights at the resort."

"You've never brought that woman here," her mother said, showing a trace of the sternness with which she once established control. "I introduced you to Matthew."

Emily laughed nervously at being upstaged. "You never asked to meet her. You look great, Mom. I expected Matthew to be here."

"He will be soon enough." But her mother was not to be deterred. "Bring her to dinner tonight."

"Mom, you don't know what's going on out there," she protested, realizing that Shelley would want to go home.

Her mother had been washing vegetables at the sink. She turned and looked at Emily. "I've heard there's been trouble. I worry about you. I'd like to meet her."

This was her mother talking? But then they'd never spoken of what it was people feared or why she might be in danger. "Shelley works in the Antique Mill on weekends."

"The men who own that place are homosexuals."

149

"So am I, Mom, and they're my friends." She could hardly believe they were having this conversation. Her heart was beating out of control. She put her hand on her chest to calm it.

"Let's go over there now. I've been wanting to see the place."

"I thought Matthew was due any minute."

"I'll leave a note for him."

Shelley looked up with surprise, glancing from one face to the other. She got up from her chair behind the desk and met them halfway with her hand outstretched.

"You must be Mrs. Hodson. The resemblance is remarkable."

Emily's mother smiled and shook hands. "The name's May."

They were the only ones in the shop, and Emily watched them as objectively as she could. It wasn't that she'd tried to keep them apart. She simply hadn't thought to bring them together. Her heart still resided in her throat, caught there like a lump.

"I wanted to invite you both to dinner tonight," her mother said.

"Can I take a raincheck? My uncle's snowmobile was stolen. I worry when I'm away too long."

"I heard. This is a small town and news gets around fast. People around here value their snowmobiles as much as their guns and trucks."

"Amen," Emily remarked wryly.

"Walt will catch whoever did it," her mother promised.

"I hope so," Shelley said without much conviction.

"I'll tell you what," her mother said while Emily held her breath. "Now that I know where you are, I'll come visit you." She glanced around. "An interesting place."

"Good. Sometimes it's lonely here."

As they climbed back in the Geo, her mother said, "She doesn't seem any different than anyone else. You'd never guess."

"Would you with me?"

Her mother turned a puzzled face toward her. "Of course not. You're my daughter."

XVII

Joe phoned one day in early December when Shelley had just returned home from Stop'n Shop. She was dead on her feet, ready to give notice. One couldn't work seven days a week and not burn out, she thought, but she was in cinders after only a few weeks.

"Hey, Mom, how's it going?"

"Good." Except for Shit'n Stuff, which was what she called Stop'n Shop, it was. "And you?"

"I called to see if you wanted me under your tree

at Christmas." He'd spent Thanksgiving with his father.

"Of course."

"Anything happening?"

"I'll tell you when I see you. How's the master's program?"

"When I see you."

She puttered around the kitchen while snow fell outside the windows. The lake was iced over. Seeing Fred drive in, she turned on the outside light, put on a jacket, and stepped into the cold. Shadows stretched across the snow.

Hugo jumped all over Fred, who grinned wolfishly as he got out of his old truck. "You'll be riding that sled after this."

She shook her head. "It was stolen."

"What?" His face darkened.

"And my largest pines were cut down."

"Why didn't you say something?"

"I thought it was general knowledge."

"Nobody tells me nothing," he grumbled. He climbed back in his truck and cleared the driveway of snow before leaving.

At supper Emily said, "People laugh at Fred, their kids run from him. No one takes him seriously."

"I do. I couldn't run this place without him."

"And maybe that's why he's loyal to you." Emily shrugged.

"Do you think he's lonely?" She thought how lonesome her uncle must have been and how lucky she was to have Emily.

"I don't know."

"Joe's coming for Christmas."

"So is Todd. He's staying at my place." Emily leaned forward, her blue eyes glittering in the candlelight. "I don't want to spend Christmas like I did Thanksgiving."

"Maybe your mother will go to Matthew's place."

"I'll suggest it. She wants to invite us all to dinner."

"I think it's amazing the way your mother seems to think I'm okay."

"My dad wouldn't have." Emily's smile was wry. "Mom's just given up on me and regards you as a huge step up from Barbara, which you are."

"A backhanded compliment if I ever heard one. What would your father say?"

"That we're perverted, that we just need a couple of good men to set us straight."

"Really?" The thought disturbed Shelley.

Emily appeared thoughtful. "I don't know. I could never see my dad objectively. We rallied around him like he was the sun."

"That's the way it is with fathers." Hers too had been the object around which her family orbited when she was young. "Mothers get the short shrift."

"Mothers usually put fathers on that pedestal and keep them there."

"And then they resent it. You sound like Jan." But Emily lacked the fervor that Jan brought to her beliefs. Emily was pointing something out, not attempting to change it.

"Have you heard from her?"

"Jan? She called a couple of weeks ago. I forgot to tell you. She finished the budget I asked her to do

for me. Said she'd mail it. Mary moved in with her."
She'd tried to picture Mary in the apartment, doing
the ordinary, everyday things with Jan that she'd
once done.

"I told her about the trees. She said I should
move into town." Like everyone else had. "It seemed
as if we were never together. That was so strange."

She felt a now familiar twinge of desire. "Want to
go huddle in bed together?"

Emily smiled and then laughed. "You're a lustful
woman."

Chicory Falls had been made festive, its light
poles laced with garlands and hung with trumpeting
golden angels. The blue spruce on the park corner
was draped with strings of brightly colored lights.

Emily was taking a teller's place around noon
when Fred shuffled up to her window. He gave off a
peculiar odor, which she associated with dirt.

"Hey, Fred. How are you?"

Plunking down a small pile of rumpled bills, he
peered at her through bloodshot eyes. "Ain't too bad.
How about yerself?" He scratched at the thick
stubble on his face.

"Okay. Where do you want me to put this
money?" She picked it up, straightening the bills.

"Savings." His large, rough hands rested on the
countertop. "Heard anything about Shelley's snowmobile?"

She lost count. "No. Have you?"

"Nope. Maybe somebody just borrowed it."

The teller was making her way back toward her window. "Why would anyone do that?"

He shrugged. His hulking figure aroused distasteful glances from employees and customers alike.

When she returned to her office, Bill knocked on the open door and walked in. Some days, like this one, he locked up the antique shop and brought leftovers to share with her at lunchtime.

"Saw Fred leaving. He sure is a strange one, isn't he? Said about two words to me."

"He's not much of a talker. What have you got today?"

He set a couple of Tupperware containers on her desk. "Parsnip soup with oyster crackers on the side."

"Beats the hell out of my bagel," she said, spooning some into her mouth. "Mmm. Good. How's business?"

"Busy on weekends. I've been trying to get Shelley to quit that job at Stop'n Shop so that I can go on a buying trip. Think you can convince her?"

"She hates working there. One big snowstorm will change her mind."

"She could stay above the store with you the days she works in town here. Why aren't you moved in together anyway?"

"What are you going to do for help in the summer, when you really need it?"

"I'll buy in the winter and work in the shop myself summers."

"How's Ted?"

"Good. You didn't answer my question about you and Shelley."

"I'm not ready to move in yet." Was it the

intimacy Shelley demanded that put her off? At any rate, she needed a little distance to feel safe.

"It's got to do with everybody dying or leaving, doesn't it, honey?" he asked, sympathetically reaching for her hand.

Knowing that her friendship with Bill and Ted set her apart as much as her friendliness toward Fred, she glanced out the door. The question rattled her.

"I don't think so."

"Sure it does. First your sister, then your father, then Barbara running off with the goods."

"Let's talk about this another time. Okay?"

"All right. I've got to go anyway. Someone might be knocking on the door with a thousand dollars to spend." He stuffed the containers back in the bag and stood up, putting a hand on her shoulder. "Don't get up. I know my way out."

She smiled. "Thanks again. Wonderful soup."

After work she went to her apartment instead of driving out to the lake. She had been there so seldom lately that it didn't feel like home. Nowhere did. She phoned Shelley.

"I thought I'd stay home tonight."

"I'm working on dinner right now. You sure you don't want to come?"

There was nothing to eat, she realized. "Well, maybe."

Shelley turned on the outside light. She had given notice at Stop'n Shop that day. Working Thursday through Sunday at the Antique Mill would bring in enough extra money. She needed the other three days to keep up on things here. And she hated leaving the dog locked inside while she was in Crystal Lake.

Having made a few decisions that she thought would please Emily, she awaited her arrival impatiently. When Emily parked in the pool of light, she pulled her inside.

"What?" Emily looked slightly annoyed.

"I quit at Shit'n Stuff."

Emily took off her jacket and hung it on the coat rack. "Funny, Bill and I were just talking about that today. He'll be pleased."

"I thought you would be too."

"I am. What does it mean?"

"The estate will be settled soon. There's not much there, though. A few thousand in savings, a ten-thousand-dollar CD."

"Sounds like a lot to me." Emily sat in a kitchen chair and took off her boots. Her curly hair had darkened with winter's approach.

"Yes, I suppose." She should have known better than to belittle her inheritance in front of Emily. It wasn't that she didn't appreciate all of it, but she knew how quickly it could be eaten up.

She said, "What do you think about a compromise on sleeping arrangements? You come out here Sunday, Monday, and Tuesday nights. I'll stay above the shop with you Wednesday, Thursday, Friday, and Saturday."

Emily looked up, her blue-gray eyes widening. "What about watching over the resort?"

"I can't do that forever. I thought you'd be pleased."

"I am, of course."

"I opened a bottle of wine to celebrate." She picked up the merlot and poured.

Emily stroked Hugo's large head, which he'd laid in her lap, and stared at the glass. "Maybe we shouldn't drink during the week."

"We don't as a rule. This is a special occasion." Anger began to get the best of her. "Look, if you didn't want to come out, you should have said so."

"I did," Emily said. "I told you I was staying home, and you said —"

"I know what I said," she snapped. "You should have told me you didn't want to come."

"We do what you want to do, Shelley."

Was that true? This disagreement mystified her. "I thought the idea was to be together. That's what I want. I was trying to work out a way."

"But what about the vandalism and stealing?"

"The place is insured." She fought down panic. "You talk like you don't want us to be together."

"Not all the time. I need a little space."

"How much?" The wine tasted flat.

"A couple nights a week."

She turned away to hide her disappointment. "Whatever, Emily."

Emily changed the subject. "Fred was in the bank today. He thought somebody had just borrowed your snowmobile."

Shelley felt close to tears and said nothing.

Taking her by the arms, Emily turned her around. "Give me time, okay?"

"All the time you want, Em."

XVIII

Shelley and Joe walked on the ice along the shoreline, while Hugo, ears flopping, bounded ahead. It was Monday, December the twenty-third, and ten to twelve inches of new snow were predicted.

"I don't trust the ice yet, Joey," she said, although a few fishing shanties were already in place farther out. "It's early."

Joe was thinner, almost gaunt. She had commented on it, and he'd said he wasn't much of a cook. But he looked stressed, like he had after she'd left his dad.

"You promised to tell me about school," she said, peering into his pale face. His shock of fair hair stood every which way, the longest portion falling over his collar. Her fingers itched to rearrange it.

He gestured dismissively. "It's okay, Ma, but I don't want to work for some big city firm."

"Call me *Mom*."

His smile was teasing. "Okay."

"How was Thanksgiving?"

"Dad's new woman is nice, but like I said, she's a little young. He's wildly happy." He glanced down at her. "You asked."

She had winced. "I'm glad for him." But no one liked being replaced, especially with someone more pleasing.

"And you promised to tell me what was happening."

The dog had stopped and was looking back at them. She didn't want to worry Joe, but she told him as she'd said she would.

He stopped in his tracks and said flatly, "I'm not leaving."

"Oh, yes, you are. You're just looking for an excuse to quit school."

"True." He grinned at her. "You always read me like a book."

"The money's invested. Don't throw it away." Her feet had grown icy in her boots. She paused and looked around, noticing how winter had altered the lake. A bitter wind kicked up the snow that covered its frozen surface. The cottages around the shoreline stood deserted and exposed with no foliage to camouflage them. Hugo returned to shiver at their feet. Snow swirled around them.

"I'm freezing, and the dog's cold. Aren't you?"

They turned and started back.

"I'll get my master's, Mom, but then I want to come back. Okay?"

It filled her with joy to know that he wanted to be here where she was, even though she knew it was the place that drew him.

"Maybe I can do Fred's work when he gets too old."

Christmas day they would have dinner for six at the resort. Emily wasn't coming out tonight because of the expected snow. She planned to work until two tomorrow and then go to her mother's for the evening. Shelley had been invited to go with her, but she had declined because of Joe.

Emily expected Todd to arrive sometime tomorrow evening. Ted had appointments most of the day on Christmas Eve, and Bill planned to keep the store open until three. Everyone would be over early Christmas to spend the day. But she felt bereft without Emily's presence now.

"What will Todd do if he gets there before you?" she had asked.

"I'll leave a key under the mat."

"Can't you come over after you go to your mother's?"

"I could, I suppose." Despite Emily's claim of wanting time alone, they had been spending most nights together.

"Should we get a movie tonight?" she asked her son as the snow thickened around them.

"Naw. Let's just hang out." He opened the door, and they stepped into the unheated mudroom. Out of the wind, it felt warm to her.

Joe stoked the fire, adding logs until it blazed. He squatted in front of the flames, drinking a can of beer.

She plunked in a chair, feeling the heat of the blaze on her cold cheeks. Snow hissed against the windows.

"Hungry?" she asked.

"Always," he answered with a white grin. His eye teeth were slightly crooked. She and his father had discussed braces and had discarded the idea. They thought the imperfection made his smile more interesting.

"I'll fix something in a moment." Public Radio was playing Christmas carols. She couldn't bring herself to interrupt the tableau of fire and glowing tree within. From her haven the near blizzard outside looked safe and friendly.

The next morning twelve inches of new snow blanketed the ground as more drifted down, creating a hushed, white world. She went outside with Joe and helped shovel the drifts away from the garage. As they worked, Fred roared in, herding snow in front of his Western snow blade.

Hugo looked up from snuffling the fresh mounds and lunged through the deep snow to greet Fred. As she watched Fred thump the dog in hello, she thought a man who likes animals is a person to be trusted.

"Hey, Fred, how's it going?" Joe shouted, tossing snow on the pile next to the garage.

"Can't complain. You folks don't need nothing, do you?" he asked, looking at her.

"Nope," she said. "We don't even have to go out today." She thought of inviting him to Christmas dinner, but didn't. He wouldn't be comfortable, she told herself.

Inside she found a message on the machine from Emily and called her number at the bank. Listening to the ringing on the line, she stared out the windows at the frozen lake.

"Are you coming out tonight?" she asked.

"I don't know. Depends on Todd and how late I stay at my mother's and the weather."

"Fred is plowing us out right now."

"We'll see," Emily said.

She pictured Emily at her desk, dressed in her work clothes, sleek and professional. She wanted her to remove the covering so she could look at the Emily underneath, the one who shared her thoughts and body with her.

Over a dinner of broccoli soup, pork tenderloin with twice-baked potatoes, and salad, she asked Joe if he wanted to go to church that night.

"We can get out now." She spoke without enthusiasm. The temperature had quickly slid below zero after sunset.

"I liked it better when we were snowed in," he said.

In the end, they never found the energy to brave the frigid night and, instead, spent the evening in front of the fire, watching Christmas programs on TV.

"This is as close to church as I've been in some time," Joe said.

After dinner with her mother and Matthew, Emily returned to the apartment to find Todd sprawled in a chair in front of the television, exhausted from the drive.

"Go to her," he said when she brought out sheets for the couch. "That's where you want to be. Then I can have the bed." He lifted his brows and made a shooing motion. "Go, go."

She acquiesced happily. "All right. You know the way to the lake. Don't make me come to fetch you."

The night was glacial, the full moon appearing and disappearing among clouds that spat the snow striking the windshield of her Geo. She drove carefully, mindful of the deer that so often committed suicide by leaping gracefully into the path of oncoming vehicles.

When she unlocked Shelley's door and glanced at the kitchen clock, it was just after midnight. Undressing in the bathroom, she climbed into bed and nestled against Shelley's back, putting a cold arm around her, carefully cupping one warm breast.

"Merry Christmas, darling," she whispered as Shelley stirred into wakefulness.

"Now it is," Shelley murmured, turning to wrap her in a cozy embrace.

Sex came easily to them, and moments later Shelley lay on top of her, lifting her nightshirt, heating her breasts with her own. By then they were breathing heavily, and as always, she was amazed at how quickly they aroused each other.

The next day Ted and Bill arrived with Todd in tow, having picked him up. They brought with them the turkey, the pies and the wine. The day before Shelley had made the stuffing for the turkey and the dough for the rolls. While the turkey slowly roasted, they exchanged gifts, went for a walk on the ice-covered lake and came back to play fictionary, a game that only required a dictionary, pen and paper, and imagination. They laughed over Todd's definition of *pistole,* an obsolete gold coin. He claimed it to be a potent mixture made primarily from horse's piss that increased potency.

"And how would someone take this compound?" Bill asked.

Todd shrugged, his dark charm evident in a slight smile. "Men will swallow anything to keep it up longer."

Emily dumped the dictionary in his lap. "You find the next word."

Light snow was falling when they sat down to eat.

Shelley brought up Fred. "I thought of asking him to come, but he just wouldn't fit in."

"Wonder what he does on the holidays. Do you know, Em?" Bill asked.

"I don't know if he has any family." A mental picture of Fred with a dark, unkempt wife and wild, wiry kids who looked like him living amid piles of junk sprang to mind. She smiled.

"What is it?" Todd asked with a tentative grin.

"Nothing."

They ended the evening with quiet talk. The lights of the Scotch pine gleamed in the window, its aroma bringing summer into the room. A fire leaped behind the glass fire screen; the heat cast a glow on the nearest faces. NPR broadcast *Messiah.* When the "Hallelujah" chorus ended, all the men except Joe stood.

"Time to go?" Shelley asked.

"Once again I lived through Christmas," Todd said, "and pleasantly for a change. What are you going to do for New Year's, girls?"

"They're coming to our house," Ted answered. "You're welcome too. It'll be quiet, though."

"Thanks, and thanks for the food and company. We can say our good-byes tomorrow, Em. I'm not leaving that early."

Joe departed at eight-thirty the next morning. Shelley had thought he would stay till New Year's, but he said he had to work on his thesis.

"When will I see you again?" she asked.

"One of these weekends," he promised with a distracted smile. It was as if he were already gone.

"Are you sure everything's all right, Joey?" she asked.

"Yeah, Mom, everything's hunky-dory."

But it wasn't, she knew. He just wouldn't tell her.

Opening the shop at ten, she turned up the heat. It was a difficult building to warm, even with a new furnace. She kept an electric heater under the desk to take the chill off. Bill was leaving on a buying trip that day; he would return New Year's Eve. He had marked down the Christmas merchandise — the ornaments and Santas, reindeer and mangers, anything with a Christmas motif.

She didn't expect to be busy, but she was. Customers were waiting in their cars when she arrived.

167

While she was ringing up a sale at noon, Emily came over to share lunch with her. Hugo rose from his rug next to the desk, his tail wagging.

"He has to go out. Can you watch the place while I take him?"

"Sure," Em said.

Outside, she walked the dog with care across the dam. Ice hung in frozen splendor, capping the rushing water. Snow lay heavily on evergreens, their branches drooping under its weight. The sky was a blue bowl, the sunlight blinding against the snowy surface, but the temperature remained stuck on zero. They hurried back to the shop.

Emily was talking to a heavy woman who was dressed in black polyester pants and a sweatshirt that proclaimed WISCONSIN WINTERS ARE FOR THE BIRDS.

Gesturing at Shelley, she said, "June Jablonski, Shelley Benson. Junie and I went to school together."

"All twelve years. She was the smart one." June grinned. "I heard about your troubles at the resort."

Shelley looked from June to Emily, wondering if June had been the pretty one. Emily outshone her now, but then Emily hadn't given birth to a pack of kids. "Do they have any leads about the snowmobile or the trees?"

"Oh, Walt doesn't talk business with me," June said. She picked up a Santa ornament and looked at it. "Isn't that cute? Not cheap, though." She put it down. "I just dropped in to see what's on sale. Stop by and see me one of these days, Em. Winter drags."

"I will," Emily promised.

Part IV

XIX

Shelley remembered June's comment later, the one about winter dragging. In the city there was always something to do. If you got bored, you went to a movie, a play, a concert, a wide array of restaurants. Here you rented a video, visited a friend, read a book, cross-country skied, ate at a supper club. By mid-February, she had seen enough snow to last her until next winter. The driveway tunneled through white drifts. Pine branches cracked under the weight of it. Unlike its city counterpart, the hinterland snow was clean and so white that she squinted against the glare. The snow muffled sound, except on cold, clear nights when the sap froze in the trees and explosive sounds like gunfire split the air.

It was Monday when she luxuriated in time for herself. She cooked for the week ahead, cleaned and filled the feeders. A flock of evening grosbeaks had arrived, devouring in one day the sunflower seeds she had put out. She read or wrote letters and caught up on her book work.

The thermometer hovered around freezing; everything being relative, it felt almost springlike outside. The porch was closed off. After Emily left for work, she sat on the living room couch with a cup of coffee and a book. Hugo lay on the flame-retardant rug in front of the fire. His hair would feel hot to the touch, she knew, but he wouldn't move from that spot.

Early afternoon she became restless and went outside with the dog. Her cross-country skis and poles were jammed into a snowbank outside the back door along with Emily's. After putting them on, she glided through the woods on the trail they had forged. Globs of snow fell on her as she brushed the pine branches in passing.

Ahead, Hugo began barking as he did when he treed a squirrel. Without hurrying she poled her way toward the sound. She heard the snarling and saw, impossibly, a red fox snapping at Hugo's nose. The dog lunged and backed off.

"Hugo, come," she shouted, thinking the fox must be rabid. Why else would it not run away?

When she realized the fox was held there by a steel leghold trap and saw the surrounding snow fanned away from the fox's desperate attempts to free itself, its trapped leg bloodied and wet, she felt a hot flash of rage. How dare someone set traps on her property without her permission? As if she would give it, she thought, staring at the animal. Backed up against the chain that kept the trap in place, its ears were pinned, its teeth bared, its tail tucked under its belly.

Now what should she do, she wondered, holding the dog by his collar. How would she open the trap and release the fox without being bitten? Removing her skis, she dragged Hugo toward the house. She'd call Bill. He was home this week.

"Are you there?" she asked impatiently when he made no immediate response.

"I'm thinking what to do. Should I get Fred?" Fred had no phone.

"No. Come now, please," she begged, certain the fox felt terror and pain as she would.

Suddenly decisive, he said, "I'll get my welding gloves and put on my heavy work jacket." Bill welded shapes out of used machinery parts. They sold well at the shop.

She paced while awaiting his arrival. Upon hearing his car, she pulled on her jacket and gloves and went outside to meet him. Shut inside, Hugo barked.

"I got here as fast as I could." He buttoned the sheepskin jacket and put the long welding gloves in his pockets. "Lead the way," he said, gesturing toward the woods.

She kept turning toward him as they trudged through the snow. "This is worse than the trees, and who cares about the snowmobile?" She became madder the more she talked. "Will you help me look for other traps? After? If there's one, there're probably more."

When they came upon the snarling fox, Bill paled, and she knew he was afraid. "Give me your coat and gloves. I'll do it."

"No. We're both going to have to do this. Let's put a rope around its neck, so it doesn't bite me in the face. Poor thing. It must be nearly mad with pain and fear." He pulled a loop of clothesline out of his jacket pocket and, from a distance, maneuvered it over the fox's head and handed her the loose end. "Keep it taut. Stretch him out between us."

She did as she was told, distracting the fox so that it chewed on the rope.

Bill got on his knees, all the while talking quietly to the frenzied animal, and forced the trap open. Then in one quick motion he slipped the noose off over the fox's head and stood up.

A moment or two passed before the fox realized it was free.

"Go on," Bill said, waving the rope. The fox turned and disappeared in seconds. He grinned at her. "We men are good for something."

"You are. Thanks," she said. "Think it'll be all right?"

"It couldn't have been in that trap long. Its leg looked intact."

Together they scoured the woods for traps, finding five more. They sprung them and pulled them from their stakes. She noticed they had been placed near paths, either animal paths or the ski trail, and baited with meat.

Back at the house, the dog whined at the door.

"Hugo would have killed it," she said as Bill shrugged out of his jacket.

"Well, that's what dogs do. The fox was in Hugo's territory." He sat down and palmed his lank hair back. "I was scared. You know? Is it too early for a drink?"

"I better call the sheriff's office first. He might want to come out or send Haines."

Bill looked doubtful. "Everyone traps around here, especially when they're young."

"How do you know? And anyway, they were trespassing." She held the receiver in one hand, looking for the sheriff's number.

"Nearly everyone who eats breakfast where I do traps."

She punched in the number. Haines answered.

"Were there any tracks?"

She tried to remember. "Did you see any footprints?" It had snowed the night before last.

Bill shook his head.

"Without tracks we're shooting in the dark. I'll come out, though. Maybe there'll be some clue."

When Emily and Ted arrived shortly after Haines's departure, Shelley said to the men, "You might as well eat here."

"Is that an invite or just resignation?" Ted asked.

She smiled. "I'm sorry. Please stay."

"You know, this might have nothing to do with anything else," Emily said.

"Haines said that whoever set those traps was riding a snowmobile. The tracks were under the last snowfall." The anger Shelley felt had given way to sadness. She could keep the traps off her land, but

175

she couldn't prevent their use on someone else's property. There was so little over which she had control.

"The thing is, people around here don't see trapping as cruel, they see it as a way to make a few extra bucks," Bill said.

"Well, we do, and we're from around here," Ted countered.

"I'm talking about the natives. In their minds trapping is connected to the old west and the mountain man," Bill went on. "They see the trapper as a self-reliant man, living off nature. A romantic figure, like the Marlboro man."

"Whose smoking killed him," Emily pointed out.

Bill shrugged. "Ah, but they don't think of that."

"I'd rather see a man in a trap. The fox was just trying to find something to eat," Shelley remarked.

"Well, nature in the buff isn't kind either," Bill pointed out. "The fox kills the quail, the wolf pulls down deer, the snake eats the frog, cats play with mice before they finish them off."

"House cats don't belong in nature," Emily said.

"Neither do dogs," Shelley added. "You should have seen Hugo. He wanted to get at that fox in the worst way." She had taken a plastic bag of panfish out of the freezer that morning, and now she rolled the fillets in a light batter and put them in the sizzling frying pan.

"Fish again," Emily said. "I'm glad I let mine go."

"So am I, but we can't waste them," she said and sighed. "I'm tired of being on the lookout all the time. Why do I have to defend what's mine?" It annoyed her that she would now have to patrol her property.

"Some people would say no one really owns the land. It should be held in trust for the next generation," Emily said.

"True." Shelley met her lover's eyes. She wasn't in the mood for an argument. "But right now I'm the caretaker of this property."

"Thanks to your uncle," Emily pointed out.

"Girls, we're all for one and one for all here. No bickering."

"Do you think it's all right for people to trap on my land, Em?" she asked, challenging where she would normally back off.

"No, of course not."

Bill and Ted exchanged a puzzled look.

The other three set the table while Shelley heaped the curled pieces of fish on a platter, removed the baked potatoes from the microwave, and popped the rolls in to warm. She handed Emily the salad.

"What is it, Em?" she asked in a low voice.

Emily shook her head. "Sorry. I don't know what got into me."

When the men were gone, Shelley asked Emily again.

Emily had a ready answer. "The attitude that owning a piece of property gives you the right to do whatever you want with it pisses me off."

"I don't feel that way, you know that," Shelley said.

"I don't know that. I told you I was sorry. It was the way you were talking about the land that struck a nerve."

Shelley sat down on the bed and looked up at her. "I never could have bought this place myself. If I hadn't inherited it, we wouldn't have met."

"And weren't you fortunate to find a lesbian nearby who was conveniently available?" Anger flared and quickly died. She hadn't even known this was still bothering her.

"I'm lucky I found you, or you found me. I'm not sure which it was." Shelley smiled so sadly that Emily, hating her own contrariness, dropped to her knees in front of the bed.

"I don't want to be a convenience."

"Why would you think you are? You know I love you."

"Do you?"

"Yes. More all the time." Shelley took her hands. "Let's go to bed. I'm exhausted."

While Shelley slept, Emily lay awake. She remembered saying last summer that if she were Jan, she would move here in a minute. Well, now she'd taken Jan's place and instead of making a commitment, she picked fights with Shelley. Bill had told her it was because of all the losses: her sister's death at an early age, her father's recent dying, Barbara's leaving and taking the goods. She didn't believe her sister's death had orchestrated her adult life, warding off intimacy. Tomorrow she would tell Shelley that she was giving up the apartment and moving into the house with her.

In the morning, though, she choked on the words,

never getting them out. She told herself that it wasn't a good month to move, that she'd do it in the spring.

"What are you going to do today?" she asked over the oatmeal Shelley had fixed for them.

"Hugo and I'll take another ski through the woods. I really want to catch the person who set those traps."

Fear flashed through Emily. "That could be dangerous."

Shelley snorted. "Yeah, well, I'm tired of being a victim. You know?"

"And what will you do if by some chance you come upon this person?" And what would she do if something happened to Shelley?

Shelley laughed. "Sic Hugo on him."

"Good idea. Hugo will lick him to death."

"What do you suggest?" Shelley arched an eyebrow.

Thinking Shelley cute, even in the morning with her hair awry and dressed in baggy sweats, she said, "Wait for the weekend. We'll look together before you go to work."

"We won't be here," Shelley said. "We'll be at your apartment, won't we?"

"No, we'll stay here." Making the decision herself gave her a sense of control.

"Let me ask you something, Emily."

"Ask quick. I'm going to be late." She took her dishes to the sink.

"Should I sell the place?"

"What?" She couldn't believe Shelley meant it and said so.

"It seems like nobody wants me to have it."

"Your son does. Remember him?" she said, meeting Shelley's cool, gray gaze. It unnerved her.

"Yes. It's keeping him from reaching for his potential."

She sat back down at the table, panicked. "You don't mean it, do you?"

Shelley nodded.

"And what would you do then?" she asked, annoyed that Shelley had brought this up now when she had to leave for work.

"I'd go to UW-Madison."

"You are serious, aren't you?" she said.

"I've thought about it more than once."

"Promise you won't do anything until we talk more about it. Okay?"

"All right."

XX

Shelley found she couldn't wait. She skied the woods Tuesday morning, shutting Hugo in the house. He would warn away an intruder. Crows cawed overhead, flying from tree to tree. Knowing the crows' penchant for harassing their natural enemies into flying, she looked for an owl or a hawk.

Adrenaline squirted painfully through her when she saw from a distance the dark figure of a man on one knee, digging in the snow. She hadn't really thought through what she would do should she find the culprit. Stepping silently off the trail into the trees, she watched as he rose to his feet and looked her way.

"Fred," she said, surprised into revealing herself, skiing his way. "Do you know who set the traps?"

He looked angry as he plowed through the snow toward her.

He did it, she thought, faltering to a stop. Here she was without even the dog to protect her. She nearly laughed. Hugo loved Fred. When he was close enough to tower over her, she attempted to clear her face of anything but surprise at seeing him.

"Why are you here?" she asked.

"Where are my traps?" His loud voice bounced off the trees. "I've trapped this land for years. What was it you let go?"

She felt almost guilty. Had her uncle given him permission to trap? "I don't want any trapping on my land," she squeaked.

"Gimme back my traps."

Haines had taken them. She told him.

He looked furious.

"Shelley." The voice, coming from behind her, sounded vaguely familiar.

She turned and saw someone in an overcoat struggling through the snow in her direction, punching more footsteps in the trail she and Emily had so assiduously created. But then Fred had already ruined the ski trail as had she and Bill and Haines. Fred! She swung around and saw that he was gone. Her heart pounded laboriously.

She skied toward the house. Gliding out of the woods and down the slight slope to the driveway, she stepped out of the skis and carried them over her shoulder. A Buick Riviera was parked in front of the garage, its exhaust blackening the snow behind it.

A man stood next to the car; the other got out of the passenger side — her brothers, whom she hadn't seen since her mother's death.

"So you are home."

"What a surprise," she said, baffled by their unannounced appearance.

"We're on a mission." Josh, the older, the one who had called her name, smiled.

"Nice place," Peter remarked, looking around.

"Thanks. Come on in." She stuffed the skis and poles in the snowbank.

In the kitchen, she made more coffee before she took off her jacket. She regretted that she hadn't taken the time to shower that morning. Her hair was flattened against her head where it wasn't flying out in electric leaps.

Her brothers wore suits. Josh was a wiry, balding man. Peter, the taller of the two, also showed signs of losing his hair.

"This is such a surprise," she repeated.

"We wanted to have a family get-together, and you have the ideal spot," Peter said, patting Hugo, who put a huge paw on his suit leg.

She snapped her fingers. "Hugo, come lie down."

"He's okay."

Josh leaned over and scratched behind Hugo's ears. The dog left Peter and placed his head on Josh's well-dressed thigh.

The two men looked at each other.

"You tell her," Peter said.

"Jean, my wife, she had a mastectomy over Christmas."

"I'm sorry, I didn't know," she murmured, still digesting their being here.

"That's the point." Josh smiled. "We've drifted so far apart. I looked up Peter, and together we came to see you."

Her mind's eye flicked through the reservation book. "How many people are we talking about?"

"We'll camp if you don't have any openings," Peter said.

"Nonsense. You can stay here at the house or in the cabins, depending on when and how many."

There were four in Peter's family, five in Josh's, and she had only one son. But of course she had Emily, too. Did they know?

"Let me get the book," she said, when they suggested Memorial Day weekend. She blocked in two cabins for them.

"We'll pay the going rate," Josh promised.

"Oh no, you won't. This is a great idea. I wish I'd thought of it."

Peter thumped Hugo's side. "We won't come if you won't let us pay."

"You're family," she said.

"Resurrected," Josh pointed out.

"Can you spend the day, at least?" She wanted them to see her after she showered, when she looked presentable.

They left after lunch.

Taking Hugo with her, she drove into town to see Haines.

"Ms. Benson, how are things going?" he asked, putting his sandwich down and standing up.

"I met Fred in the woods. I don't know if my uncle gave him permission to trap. But he wants his traps back. Please tell him not to set them on my land."

At the bank she sat in one of the chairs in Emily's office and told her all that had happened that day, starting with Fred.

"Why couldn't you wait till Saturday? He might have hurt you."

"Why would he?" Doubt crept into her voice as she pictured Fred towering angrily over her.

"Maybe your brothers saved you."

"Em, I need Fred." How would she open the resort without him? How would she maintain it? "Everything has to be ready by Memorial Day weekend. The water needs to be turned on to the cottages. I don't think I remember how to do that."

Emily said nothing. She rocked back in her chair.

"I'm going to need your help, Em."

"I know less than you do," Emily said.

Emily watched Shelley walk through the lobby and out the door. A prickling sensation crawled up her arms and back as she thought of Fred living in that falling down house surrounded by junk. Shelley assumed he was on her side. Perhaps, instead, he used his position to profit himself.

She stopped at her mother's after work. Matthew was watching the news on TV. Her mother came to the kitchen door when she walked in.

"Hello, stranger," Matthew said.

She got to the point. "Matthew, what do you know about Fred Winslow?"

"He's a strange one."

"We all know that," she said.

"Why, dear?" her mother asked.

She told them.

Matthew said, "I used to run the hardware store. I went to all the lakes, opening cottages. I can help Shelley when the time comes. She doesn't have to depend on Fred."

"You'd do that?" she said.

"Sure. Why not?"

"Will you stay for dinner, Emily?" her mother asked.

"I can't, Mom. Thanks, Matthew."

After five, the sun dropped swiftly, taking with it the little warmth it offered. In the dark of the moon a star-filled sky and the snowy fields and ditches offered the only light. The tunneled driveway reminded her of Fred's essentialness. Matthew didn't plow snow.

Pulling around the sheriff's car, she drove into the

garage and parked next to Shelley's Bronco. The night was still and cold. She hurried inside.

Haines and Jablonski were in the kitchen talking with Shelley. Hugo barked once with joy and nosed her in welcome.

"You know Emily Hodson, don't you?" Shelley said.

"Sure do. She lived down the block from us. Her and my wife went to school together."

"Hi, Walt." She nodded at Haines. "Hello."

"They found my snowmobile out in a field in good, running condition. Somebody just left it there." Shelley's gray eyes were somber.

"No prints on it. Nothing."

"Fred?" she asked.

Shelley shrugged. "Could've been."

"Might not have been either," Jablonski said. "All we can do is keep an eye on him. Like Shelley said, her uncle might have given him leave to trap."

"You don't want him trapping anymore, though. Right?" Haines cut in.

"I don't trust him anymore. You gave him back his traps?" Shelley looked at the two men.

"Yep. Told him not to set them here again."

"You know anybody who plows snow?" Emily asked.

"My oldest boy, Ronnie," Walt said.

Shelley looked alarmed. "How am I going to tell Fred that somebody else is going to plow the drive?"

"I'll tell him," the sheriff said.

"No, not until I'm sure he's guilty of anything more. I hired him; I'll fire him when I'm ready."

"You inherited him," Emily pointed out.

"Well, it's up to you," Jablonski said. "We got to get going. That good smell is making me hungry."

"Say hello to June," she said, going to the door with Shelley as they left.

"Come on, Hugo," Shelley called when the dog slipped outdoors with the men. He barked once and ran back inside.

When they sat down to eat, Emily told Shelley that Matthew would help her open the cottages. "You can replace Fred. Why don't you tell him you can't afford him?" She felt Hugo's body snubbed up against her toes under the table.

Shelley met her eyes. "You should have seen how angry he was. I'm afraid to fire him. I'm a coward."

Goose bumps spread across her arms and legs. "Promise me you won't go into the woods alone."

"I promise, not without Hugo."

The dog crawled out from under the table and gave them such a hopeful, hungry look that Shelley gave him a Milk-Bone dog biscuit.

Most work nights Emily wanted only to read or talk in bed. That night she snuggled up to Shelley as Shelley opened her book.

"Want your back scratched?" she offered.

"Already?" Shelley asked, turning obligingly onto her belly.

Emily pressed her cheek against Shelley's shoulder and whispered, "I wouldn't want to live here without you."

"I wouldn't want to live anywhere without you," Shelley muttered into the pillow.

When it was her turn, Shelley pressed against the length of Emily's back. "Want to?" She kissed Emily's shoulder blades and the nape of her neck. She ran a hand lightly down her spine and between her legs.

"You have to warm your fingers first."

Making love under the covers, they quickly overheated and threw off the layers.

"Move in, Em," Shelley said, holding her close.

"In the spring," she promised, her blood pounding in the aftermath.

XXI

It sometimes snowed in April, Shelley knew, but no matter. To her spring had arrived with the returning birds — the sandhill cranes clacking through the skies, the redwing blackbirds shirring for mates, the robins pecking at the ground, the geese honking overhead, the ducks on the wing. The lake ice had broken up, piling onto the shore. Now she understood why people took out their piers. It wasn't the winter ice that destroyed them, it was the spring thaw.

She dragged out the metal chair and sat on it near the water while Hugo cavorted. Except to dash in and out, even he found the water too icy to enjoy. Another two weeks and it would be May, when she'd first arrived here a year ago. With money in the savings and reservations coming in, she felt a deep satisfaction.

It was after five on a Wednesday, at the end of a sunny day. Having tired from raking, she was awaiting Emily's arrival, wanting to relax with a glass of wine near the water. Hearing the approach of a vehicle, she saw Hugo stretch into a run.

Expecting Emily to come to her before going inside, she swiveled around when enough time had passed. She saw Fred's pickup parked near the garage. Her heart thumped unhealthily as she got up and started toward the vehicle. She had told Fred at the end of March, about the time that Emily moved in with her, that she didn't need him anymore. So what was he doing here? And where were he and Hugo?

The two of them came out of the house as she approached, and she developed an instant headache. She thought she might puke at Fred's feet. Where the hell was Emily?

"What were you doing in the house, Fred?"

He looked around with red-streaked eyes. "Looks like you kin use a hand."

"I told you, Fred, I can't afford you."

He brushed her words aside as if she hadn't spoken and strode toward the garden tractor and trailer. "I'll take care of this."

She hurried to keep up with him. "I can't pay you, Fred."

"Pay me when you kin." He was climbing on the little tractor, turning the key. The engine caught. "I'll unload this stuff."

"Damn," she said as he drove off toward the edge of the woods where they piled leaves and brush.

"What's Fred doing here?" Emily asked.

She jumped. "Where did you come from?"

"I just got home. What's going on?"

"I told him I didn't need him anymore. You heard me. Did I make it clear?" she said, wondering what to do.

"It was clear to me. Maybe you better call Haines."

Across the drive, Fred put the John Deere in neutral and started kicking the contents off the open tailgate of the trailer. Hugo, who was with him, saw Emily and bounded toward her.

"Oh, sure. I'll ask Haines to fire him for me." She looked pleadingly into Emily's blue-gray eyes. "You tell him, Em."

Hugo reached Emily and leaned against her in greeting. "Okay. I will," she said, heading toward Fred who'd driven the tractor and trailer around the side of the house.

Shelley followed.

"Hi, Fred." Emily reached for the key, turning off the machine. She cleared her throat in the silence that followed.

Fred was looking at them, his thick brows drawn together in displeasure. He needed a shave. "Can't you see I'm working here?" he growled.

"That's just it, Fred. Shelley told you she had to let you go, that she can't afford you as an employee anymore."

He thumped his chest. "I keep this place running."

Shelley stepped back. She had to give Emily credit for not doing the same.

"Not anymore, Fred," Emily said gently.

"Who are you anyway? You don't own the place." He lowered his voice. He looked dangerous, and no longer in a funny way.

"Neither do you, Fred."

He threw the rake down. "Quit calling me *Fred* like that. I don't work for you."

Shelley stepped forward then and put a hand on Emily's arm. "Thanks," she said quietly. "I let you go, Fred, remember?" The dog sat between her and Emily, looking at their faces as they talked. Perhaps he sensed their vulnerability.

Fred scowled. "Look, lady, I been here since before your uncle came. He didn't know nothing, just like you. He dropped dead and gave you the place. After all I done." He stalked off toward his truck.

She held the dog by his collar until the truck was out of sight, hung on until Hugo whined. "Sorry, Hugo." She let him go. "That was scary."

"Let's hope it's the end of him," Emily said. "I'm going in to change clothes."

Trailing after Emily into the bedroom, she experienced a sense of foreboding. "What if he comes back? What if he never leaves?"

"Why don't you call Haines and talk to him?"

Stretching out on the bed, she watched Emily

strip off her work clothes and put on sweats. "Haines is probably gone for the day. I wanted to sit on the beach and share a glass of wine with you."

"Just like old times," Emily said.

But then Joe called. "Mom, I'm coming home this weekend."

"Why don't you wait till May, Joey, when I won't be working at the shop on weekends?" Instead, the resort would require all her energy.

"I have to talk to you."

"Talk. I'm listening."

"In person," he said.

"All right, son. We'll find time to squeeze in a few conversations."

When they finally went outside with the dog and their wine, the sun was a red orb sinking into the wetlands. There was no wind, but neither was it warm. Bundled in jackets, they sat near the shore.

"Think you'll miss this quiet?" Emily asked. "Summer means the phone ringing, people knocking on the door, boats being launched. We'll have no privacy."

"You should have moved in months ago. We would be sick of each other by now maybe."

"Fat chance. We were living together anyway; it just wasn't official. I hadn't given up the apartment or put my stuff in the same closet."

"Your apartment is now filled with antiques, so you can't move back."

"I wasn't planning to."

"Listen," she said, shushing Emily. The faint

chirring of chorus frogs reached their ears and quickly died.

The next morning Emily reminded Shelley to call Haines. They drove to town in different vehicles, because Emily had to be at work before Shelley did. She also returned home earlier.

After work, Emily stopped at the grocery store. When she turned into the driveway to the resort, there was still plenty of daylight.

Unlocking the door, she released Hugo. They were having leftovers that night, so there was no need to start dinner. She changed her clothes and went outside with the dog. This was the best part of living here, being able to walk out the door and see the lake and smell the pines.

Hugo was sniffing around cabin eight. She walked toward him, and her gaze was caught by something not quite right. As she closed in on the cabin, she saw the windows broken, the door bashed in. She hesitated before going inside. Someone angry had done this, someone she didn't want to run into. Fred, she assumed.

But the inside was untouched, as if all the rage had been vented on the outside. She walked through the small rooms warily. When the dog padded up behind her, she turned with a start, her heart gone wild.

"Don't sneak up on me like that, Hugo."

Should she wait for Shelley to get home or see if she could still catch her at work? She decided on the latter. Shelley could notify Haines. But she was reluctant to do so, knowing that Shelley would be crushed by this. It would seem to her a personal attack.

Bill followed Shelley down the driveway, in turn trailed by Haines's car.

Emily waited with Hugo as they got out of their vehicle, then they all walked over to cabin eight.

Haines studied the ground around the door and windows. He knelt with difficulty and took imprints of the shallow indentations in the ground.

"Maybe we can get a footprint out of this," he said, looking up at them.

"Fred," Shelley said. "How could he, after all the work we put into these cabins?"

Bill put his arm around Shelley, and Emily turned away and squinted at the lake, not seeing it really, but instead wondering if they could continue to live this way, never knowing what they would discover when they came home.

Haines left, promising to call with his findings.

"Do you think I should sell, Bill?" Shelley asked when they went inside so that Bill could phone Ted.

"Not because of this," he said.

Emily picked up Hugo's food bowl. He tap-danced on his toenails while she filled it with Purina and poured warm water over it. "If we pool our money, Shell, we should be all right no matter what happens."

"You would do that, Emily?"

"I love it here."

"If I went back to college and got my degree, we

could buy a spot on a lake and not have to work ourselves to death."

"Maybe it won't be so much work with me living here and helping," she said, wondering if it was wrong to discourage Shelley from selling, from going back to school.

"What would you major in?" Bill asked.

Shelley snorted. "I don't know. And I'd be over fifty when I graduated. Not a good age to be looking for a job."

"You've got a ready-made business of your own," Bill pointed out.

Shelley brightened. "You're right. I'd be foolish to sell and spend all the money getting a degree so that I could work for somebody else."

"When you sell this place, you should retire with the money," Bill said.

"Right you are. But first I have to fix cabin eight."

"It was our cabin. We'll help."

"Do you know anything about construction?" Shelley asked.

"Sure. And I'll work this weekend. Joe's coming, right?"

Emily felt a tremendous relief.

They slept restlessly that night, waking at every noise. Emily placed a hand on the small of Shelley's back as Shelley lay on her stomach. The feel of Shelley's skin soothed her, the contact anchored her. She'd fought the closeness Shelley represented, even as she wondered why, and she knew she would continue battling her fear of intimacy.

The next morning Emily awoke tired. Shelley was gone from the bed. She shuffled to the kitchen, poured herself a cup of coffee and took it to the shower.

Before leaving for work, she went outside where Shelley was looking at the damaged cabin. Hugo greeted her joyously.

"I hate leaving you here," she said.

"I'll be fine." Shelley smiled tiredly. "You didn't sleep well either, did you?"

She shook her head, looking around. The morning promised a warm day. She wished she could stay here, at least until she knew Shelley's state of mind.

"You all right, Shell?"

"I think so. It helps to know that you're behind me."

Emily felt guilty, knowing that sometimes she must seem adversarial. "I always am. I try to be anyway."

XXII

Joe stood with Shelley, looking at the broken windows and door of cabin eight. "Jesus, Mom, who did this?"

She hesitated, then said, "Could have been Fred."

He frowned at her. "Fred! Why would he?"

"I fired him."

Joe stared at her. "You let him go because he was trapping on the property without your permission?"

"I don't trust him anymore, Joey. He might be the one who cut the trees, planning to sell them for pulp. He probably stole the snowmobile and then abandoned it in a field when it was too hot to keep."

His sandy hair lifted in the slight breeze. "Can you get along without him?"

She told him about Matthew's offer to turn on the water to the cabins. "I'll learn how to do those things myself."

"I'll learn with you. I'm here to stay," he said.

"But you don't have your master's yet."

"I'm not going to finish. That's what I came home to tell you." His gaze fixed on the lake, its blue surface ruffling in a fickle breeze.

She said, "But why, Joey?"

"I'm HIV positive," he said.

At first she thought she had misheard him, but her reaction was immediate and physical. Sweat popped out over her skin, her heart pounded in her ears, vomit climbed her throat. She swallowed rapidly. "When —"

"I don't know when, I don't know who. I don't have AIDS, Mom." He spoke gently, as if to comfort her. "But the way things are, it's just a matter of time. And I want to spend that time here."

She fell speechless. He was her only child, whom she loved fiercely. Her throat and nose filled with tears, and she gulped them down. Parents aren't supposed to live longer than their children.

"Have you told your dad?" she finally asked.

"No, and I don't want you to either. He doesn't need to know yet."

Oh, Joey, she thought, he has to prepare himself too. And then she realized he would probably have ample time.

Joe held himself stiffly, his head high, as if fighting his own demons.

She nodded, not trusting her voice, thinking, no wonder we don't want our sons to be gay.

"Mom, it's not the end of the world." He put an arm around her shoulders and hugged.

A tiny sob escaped her, followed by another.

Joe wrapped her up tight. The sounds of their crying mingled with the nearby frogs.

Emily sat through dinner with Joe and Shelley, both subdued, knowing something was terribly wrong.

"I'll tell you later," Shelley said when Joe went out for a walk with Hugo.

Now they were in bed, whispering in the dark, while Joe lay in the other room.

"He's positive?" she asked just to make sure she'd heard Shelley right. A coldness crept through her.

"Yes." Shelley's voice cracked. She began to cry, choking as she tried to swallow the noise.

"Hey, it's okay." The sudden gust of emotion rattled her. She gathered Shelley up and rocked her. "I'm so sorry."

"I can't stop c-c-crying."

"It's okay. Cry." She kissed Shelley's hair and cheeks, tasting the salt. Using the sheet, she wiped away the tears as they fell. "But you know, he may be fine for years."

Shelley sniffed and took a deep, shuddering breath. "Do you think I should encourage him to finish his degree?"

"I don't know. What is he going to do here? It's pretty boring in the winter."

"I didn't ask him. Somehow nothing else seemed important."

"I suppose not," she said, thinking about what it would be like here year-round for Joe. "Well, I imagine he needs to hole up somewhere right now. Maybe he could write his thesis here. Is he through with classes?"

"I have no idea. It must seem pretty pointless."

She was thinking you never know when you're going to be struck down. It could happen anytime, to any of them. But it wasn't the same, she knew. Being HIV positive was like being told you had inoperable cancer. Worrisome thoughts churned around her head. Was Todd guilty of infecting Joe? She had introduced them, encouraged them. Should Roger be told? How could they possibly do that without disseminating the information? That would make them popular here. The acts of vandalism committed against the resort were minor compared to what might follow.

She would have to call Todd.

At work Monday Emily left a message with Todd's receptionist for him to phone her at work, not at home. She tried to concentrate on business but found herself doodling on sheets of paper. Over the lunch hour she walked to the antique shop. Spring was in the air; newly green grass was sprouting and leaves uncurling; birds were singing. The store was closed, but Bill was arranging the antiques he'd bought while away. She pounded on the locked door.

"Hey, girlfriend, what's up?" He let her in, a dust rag in his hand. "How's Shelley doing? I'm going to see her today."

"The cabin isn't the worst thing by far," she said, closing and locking the door behind her.

"What?"

He paled as she spoke and sat with a thump on the nearest chair. "Christ! What a fucking mess. Poor Joe."

"Poor Shelley," she said. "She's so sad, almost defeated."

"I'll go out there right now," he said. "First I'll call Ted."

She looked down at him sitting in the old morris chair and was so glad he was part of their lives. "I need some advice. I've got a call into Todd, but what about Roger?"

"Like dominoes, isn't it? First you need to find out if Todd is positive. Joe didn't see Roger after Todd, did he?"

"Is this our business?"

"I think so," he said with a sigh. "I'll talk to Joe."

When she returned to the bank, there was a message from Todd. She closed her door and punched in his number. Was she jumping the gun? But he was her good friend, and she was already implicated.

"Todd, how are you?"

"I didn't know, Em. Honest."

She swiveled her chair and stared unseeing at the parking lot. "I believe you. I'm sorry, Todd."

203

"Me too," he said. "Joe stopped by last week."

"Did he have anything to do with Roger after you?"

"Ask him." There was a pause. "You could be opening a can of worms, you know. There's life after being found positive, often years of it."

It occurred to her that maybe Joe had given the virus to Todd. They'd never know, and in the end, did it matter?

"Em, I've got a reservation there this summer. I'll see you then?" It came out as a question.

"Okay, Todd. Take care of yourself."

Shelley felt flattened by the events of the past week. When she looked at Joe, she fought off tears. The cabin became a diversion for her, something to distract her from Joe's news.

Early afternoon Bill drove in. She and Hugo greeted him. Joe had left before noon without saying where he was going.

He gave her a hug. "I'm sorry, Shell."

Burying her face in his bony shoulder, she cried. When she could talk, she said, "I feel like I've offended God."

"I didn't know you believed in a god."

"You think it's all chance?" she asked.

He wiped her face dry, then walked with her toward the beach. "I haven't a clue. I can't believe any god would orchestrate something like AIDS. But Joe doesn't have AIDS. He's positive." He glanced toward cabin eight.

"I know. I have to get a grip on myself and stop crying all the time." Her head and eyes ached. She followed his gaze and sighed. "I don't know if I want them to nail Fred or not."

"If he's guilty, why not?"

She sniffed at the soft breeze. It was April at its best, burgeoning with the promise of renewed life, but the sterility of winter was in her heart.

"We're all to blame." She walked toward the metal chair and the molded plastic one next to it.

He followed her. "For what?"

"Whatever we do affects someone."

"And what did you do to Fred?"

"I took what he thought should be his," she said.

"Come on, Shell. It was never his."

"Anyway, we don't know if he did this or cut the trees or took the snowmobile."

"Ten to one he did," he said. "We'll fix the cabin as soon as possible."

She smiled. "You and Ted are good friends."

"You'll have to feed us and provide us with something to drink." He touched her hand.

"I've got to stop this," she said, breaking into sobs.

"You will."

They sat quietly in the sun, Hugo stretched out at their feet, listening to the frogs and the spring peepers, watching the lake move and glisten. If not peace, she experienced the certainty of knowing that life continued around her.

At dinner that night they regrouped. Bill had spent the remainder of the day with Shelley. Ted came over after work, arriving at the same time as

Emily. Joe told them he had his job back at the gas company starting the end of May. Until then he would help ready the resort for summer.

As he had promised, Bill talked to Joe. There was no need to tell Roger anything, Joe assured him.

"Thank God," Emily said, when Bill told her. "Imagine if that leaked out in town."

Matthew came out on Sunday at the end of April to turn on the water to the other cabins, putting the plugs back in the lines, filling the small water heaters and the toilet tanks, getting the air out of the plumbing. He brought her mother with him. Shelley asked them to stay for supper. Matthew would accept no money.

She was glad now that her mother had Matthew. It meant that she needn't worry about her being lonely. She had read somewhere that widows who had enjoyed a good marriage remarried. Not that her mother had mentioned marrying Matthew, but she figured that was coming next.

During a meal of hamburgers on the grill, baked beans, and potato chips, which they all ate outside in the cooling evening, Shelley apologized. "We'll have you over when it's not so hectic around here. I'll fix a real meal for you."

Matthew said, "Not for me. This is just great. Everything always tastes so much better when it's grilled and eaten outside. Right, May?"

"Yes. It's wonderful," her mother said gamely as she huddled in a jacket.

She smiled to herself. How different her mother

was from the woman she'd come home to after her father's death. Maybe she required a man to make her shine. Perhaps everyone needed someone to bring out the best part of them.

XXIII

He might outlive her, Shelley thought, eyeing Joe carefully so that he wouldn't catch her looking. There had to be stats that traced people who were HIV positive. Perhaps some people never developed full-blown AIDS.

He looked so clean muscled and healthy with his shirt off in the warm day. Leaning on the rake, he said, "Mom, stop studying me like a specimen or something. I'm not going to drop dead for a long time."

"That's not funny, Joey."

"Let's pretend I never told you I was positive. Okay? Treat me like you always have. Anyway, I'm not going to get AIDS." He was grinning. His shock of hair already turning its summer white, his freckles dark against a beginning burn, his eyes bright.

She flinched. "I'm trying, Joey."

"Try harder."

"I am," she snapped.

He laughed. "That's more like it."

But the truth was she carried the knowledge wrapped around her heart, where it tightened into a painful knot whenever it came to mind. If she could forget, she would. At first the what-ifs kept her awake nights; now she escaped into sleep quickly and dreamed in vivid colors. All she remembered when she woke up were the reds, oranges, yellows, purples.

She supposed that with time she would become used to it. "Did you ever worry about this happening?" she asked.

"I thought we were going to forget it, not dredge up the details." He turned his head toward the water. The dog barked and dropped a stick at his feet.

As he threw for Hugo, he said, "Yes, no, sometimes. I thought of it. You just don't expect stuff like this to happen to you. It happens to somebody else."

How well she knew. If it had been easy for her to get pregnant, she would have had children early on. She nodded.

"Roger and I never did anything but talk," he said. "I wasn't that foolish. Having you and Emily and Ted and Bill around is like having four parents sometimes. You have to remember that I'm nearly twenty-five."

And you're HIV positive, she said to herself.

"I'll tell Dad if I get AIDS," he said as if she'd brought up the subject herself. "I promise."

She nodded, wincing again and squinting at the sun on the water. "Feels good to be warm, doesn't it? To be able to go outside without a jacket?"

He was looking toward the house.

Following his gaze, she saw Fred striding across the needle-strewn ground in their direction. Hugo dropped the stick and bounded toward him.

"Hi, Fred," Joe said.

She only stared. Fred was freshly shaven, his hair shampooed, his clothes clean, but he still exuded an aura of disrepute.

He nodded at Joe and inclined his head in the direction of the cabin. "I came to fix it for you," he said. "I heard."

"It's done," she said, having meant to tell him to go away. "Where did you hear?"

"Haines," he said, looking at her angrily. "He follows me around like a damn mosquito."

"Well, that's because of the traps and the trees and the snowmobile and the cabin," she said irritably.

He stared over her head. "Somebody done you a favor. Them woods needed thinning. Didn't you sell them trees for pulp?"

"Are you saying you cut them down as a good deed?"

His fierce gaze fell on her. "There's room now for the other trees to grow. Don't you always need money?"

Joe cleared his throat. "Those trees weren't yours to cut."

"I didn't say I cut 'em. And that snowmobile

wasn't hurt none, was it? The only thing bad was breaking the windows and door on that there cabin."

And he was here to repair the damage, she thought. She'd got her confession. He wanted his job back. "Fred, I'm going to try to make do without hired help. Joe is going to work for me in his spare time. But when there's something we can't do, I'll let you know. Why don't you stop in once a week and see if we need you?" It was the best she could do.

"I just want to check out the cabin," Fred said.

A terrible sadness fell over her. She looked at Joe, who shrugged and smiled. Fred was walking toward cabin eight with Hugo running circles around him. The dog loved him. Could he be so bad?

"Want me to call Haines?" Joe asked.

She shook her head. "Let's see what he does."

Joe said, "Maybe he wanted to show you that he was indispensable by fixing the cabin."

With a rueful smile, she remarked, "Could be. But perhaps you should call Haines."

"You sure?" Joe asked. "I feel sort of sorry for him."

"Just tell him Fred's here looking at the cabin, that he came to repair it."

"Don't go near him without me," Joe warned.

"I won't." Then, "On second thought, maybe I should call Haines."

The deputy sheriff asked her if she wanted him to come get Fred.

"I don't think so. He's just looking."

"If you ever want rid of him, you can't let him show up whenever he feels like it."

"I need to know something," she said. "Has Fred ever hurt anyone?"

Haines pursed his lips. "Not to our knowledge. Why?"

"Because I don't think we can keep him away."

Emily found her mother in the kitchen, peeling potatoes. The light flowing through the window enhanced the wrinkles around her eyes and mouth. Emily felt her heart contract a little as she kissed the soft cheek that was crisscrossed with lines.

"How are you, dear?" Potato peels flew from her mother's knife and plastered themselves to the sink.

"What's the news you wouldn't tell me over the phone, Mom?"

"Matthew and I are moving in together."

"I thought maybe you were getting married," she said. "His place or yours?"

"Whichever one rents, we'll live in the other. There's not much market for rentals here."

"Why aren't you marrying him, Mom?" She'd thought appearances were important to her mother.

"I did that once, honey." A sly smile played across her mother's lips.

Emily planted another kiss on her pink cheek. "I'm glad for you."

Her mother dropped the potato and hugged her. "And I'm happy for you."

"Thanks, Mom."

"You're a good daughter," her mother added in the flush of her happiness.

"Do you really think so?" she asked, surprised.

"Yes. I'm lucky to have you."

"Rather than Ellen?" She froze, wondering where that need for reassurance had come from, worried that her mother might tell her the truth.

"Oh honey, do you think I'd give you up? If I'd been given a choice, I couldn't have made it."

Astonished to see tears in her mother's eyes, she felt her own fill and turned away from the emotion. She mumbled, "Thanks, Mom," knowing that even if her mother couldn't make the choice, Ellen would have fulfilled her parents' expectations better than she had.

Home long before dark, she changed into sweats and went outside looking for Shelley. She found her with Joe down by the boat ramp.

Hugo made it impossible to sneak up on anyone. They turned as soon as the dog streaked toward her.

"Sit down, Em, and watch the sun set." Joe smiled at her.

"Something happen?" she asked warily, knowing it had.

"Fred was back," Shelley said. "I give up."

Emily opened the folding chair. The sun shone warmly on their faces. It lit a widening path across the surface of the water.

"What do you mean you give up?" She sat down next to Shelley.

"I can't keep him away."

"Oh." She understood. It filled her with worry. At least soon the resort would open. There was safety in numbers.

"There is an option, you know. I could sell the place."

"What?" Joe said.

"Em?" Shelley looked at her.

"If you're serious, why don't you talk to a Realtor," she said, annoyed.

"Mom, you'd be crazy to sell this place."

XXIV

Shelley called a Realtor, told her she might be interested in putting the resort on the market, and asked that she come out while Emily and Joe were at work. But when the Realtor, a spindly, overly made-up woman, got there, Shelley realized it was all wrong to even think about selling on this flawless May day. How could she consider leaving when the breeze was a caress, redolent with lake and earth and new growth, when the leaves were nearly translucent in their newness, the lake blue and inviting, the birds and frogs singing their instinctive passions?

She apologized for changing her mind before she had even made it up. The Realtor said that if she changed it again to phone her.

Watching as the woman drove away, Shelley felt a sense of reprieve. She had rescued herself from doing the practical thing. Anyway, how could she move away when Joe had come home to stay? And Emily, after finally trusting her enough to move in, would have to quit her job and find one elsewhere. There were lots of reasons not to sell. Her brothers and their families would be here in a week. And she had invited Emily's mother and Matthew and his grand-children for a cookout on the Sunday of Memorial Day weekend.

Ted and Bill and Joe had put in the pier over the weekend. They'd gritted their teeth and grunted when the icy water lapped at sensitive parts. Bill had hired Em's old friend, June, to work in the antique shop every other weekend. Shelley and Emily had cleaned the cabins, readying them for guests.

Once a week she saw Fred. He checked out the motors and put them on the boats. She had a few minutes of déjà vu as he took a test run around the lake with Hugo standing in the prow.

She had gained a few extra hours by giving up mowing. She liked the sparse, tall grass better; it was soft underfoot. And she loved the wildflowers that sprang up throughout the summer when unimpeded: phlox, spiderwort, daylilies, black-eyed Susans, daisies, chicory, bergamot.

* * * * *

Friday night of Memorial Day weekend the guests began arriving. There were none to depart, so there was no reason why anyone should wait till Saturday. Shelley was standing in the yard when her brothers drove in. Hugo flattened his ears and rushed the vehicles.

The doors opened and her brothers, their wives, and children spilled from Josh's Buick and Peter's Caravan. She stared at their offspring, who were grown or nearly so, sorry that she had not made the effort to keep in touch.

Refusing their offers of money, she took them to cabins six and seven. "You take care of the food Sunday. That'll help me immensely," she told them. "There'll be ten from my side of the family." Herself, Emily, Joe, Ted and Bill, Em's mother and Matthew, Matthew's grandchildren.

Another car had driven in, an Explorer which she knew carried Jason and Shawn. "Got to go," she said.

"Drinks and snacks tonight at seven," her brother, Josh, called after her.

"I'll try," she said.

"Just like the bad pennies," Jason announced cheerfully. "We're back."

"I need those pennies," she said. "Cabin one okay?"

"Lovely," Shawn replied as Emily arrived in her new Ford Escort.

"And the missus is?" Shawn asked.

Em laughed. "I'm Emily. There is no missus. That's the best part."

"Congratulations," Jason said.

The weekend passed quickly. Shelley had forgotten

how much of her time went to paying guests. They ran out of toilet paper, needed gas, couldn't remember how to start the motors, wanted to buy bait, or simply desired to talk. She was constantly hurrying from one thing to another.

The guests brought food offerings to the cookout Sunday evening, joining Shelley and her family. She assessed them over the flames leaping in the outdoor fireplace. Her brothers and their families no longer felt like strangers.

When the fire died down, after Emily's mother and Matthew left with the grandchildren and some of the guests went to their cabins, Shelley walked to the water's edge with Emily.

Ted and Bill followed. The night was cool, the water black except for pinpoints of stars and the waning moon reflected in its surface.

Ted reminded them, "A year ago today you knocked into that tree, Em."

"And all of you rescued me," Emily said.

"It's our anniversary," Bill pointed out.

The lake slapped idly at their feet. Hugo stood up to his belly in the water, looking at them expectantly.

When Shelley made love to her, Emily often became lost in the process, but not tonight. She heard the dog scratching himself, listened to him turn around and around before lying down with a thump and a sigh, heard his feet running in his sleep.

She let Shelley take over, finding desire in being submissive in sex whereas in every other way she was not.

Her feelings for Shelley defined the act for her, made it right and natural. And she wondered how much sex was going on in the cabins at this moment.

At the fire that night she'd asked her mother who in her family had shared her proclivity for the same sex.

Her mother had whispered, "Why, your father's brother, dear. Such a fun man he was, but your dad couldn't deal with him."

She laughed softly in the dark.

"What is it, darling?" Shelley asked.

"Something my mother said. It appears you and I both had gay uncles." She turned serious. "Shelley, I'm so sorry about Joe, really I am. I love Joe, you know I do. And yet I'm happy."

"Me too." Shelley sighed and hugged her close. "Amazing how it sneaks up on you when you're not looking, isn't it? Sort of a bittersweet feeling. We can't be miserable all the time. Nobody would come here."

The summer stretched before them, a much-anticipated hiatus. Emily looked forward to every day, despite the uncertainty awaiting them. And she thought that when fall arrived, they would also be ready for winter's retreat.

A few of the publications of
THE NAIAD PRESS, INC.
P.O. Box 10543   Tallahassee, Florida 32302
Phone (850) 539-5965
Toll-Free Order Number: 1-800-533-1973
Mail orders welcome. Please include 15% postage.
Write or call for our free catalog which also features an
incredible selection of lesbian videos.

RHYTHM TIDE by Frankie J. Jones. 160 pp. . . . to desire
passionately and be passionately desired.   ISBN 1-56280-189-9 $11.95

PENN VALLEY PHOENIX by Janet McClellan. 208 pp. 2nd
Tru North Mystery.   ISBN 1-56280-200-3   11.95

BY RESERVATION ONLY by Jackie Calhoun. 240 pp. A
chance for true happiness.   ISBN 1-56280-191-0   11.95

OLD BLACK MAGIC by Jaye Maiman. 272 pp. 9th Robin
Miller Mystery.   ISBN 1-56280-175-9   11.95

LEGACY OF LOVE by Marianne K. Martin. 240 pp. Women
will do anything for her . . .   ISBN 1-56280-184-8   11.95

LETTING GO by Ann O'Leary. 160 pp. Laura, at 39, in love
with 23-year-old Kate.   ISBN 1-56280-183-X   11.95

LADY BE GOOD edited by Barbara Grier and Christine Cassidy.
288 pp. Erotic stories by Naiad Press authors.   ISBN 1-56280-180-5   14.95

CHAIN LETTER by Claire McNab. 288 pp. 9th Carol Ashton
mystery.   ISBN 1-56280-181-3   11.95

NIGHT VISION by Laura Adams. 256 pp. Erotic fantasy romance
by "famous" author.   ISBN 1-56280-182-1   11.95

SEA TO SHINING SEA by Lisa Shapiro. 256 pp. Unable to resist
the raging passion . . .   ISBN 1-56280-177-5   11.95

THIRD DEGREE by Kate Calloway. 224 pp. 3rd Cassidy James
mystery.   ISBN 1-56280-185-6   11.95

WHEN THE DANCING STOPS by Therese Szymanski. 272 pp.
1st Brett Higgins mystery.   ISBN 1-56280-186-4   11.95

PHASES OF THE MOON by Julia Watts. 192 pp. . . . . hungry
for everything life has to offer.   ISBN 1-56280-176-7   11.95

BABY IT'S COLD by Jaye Maiman. 256 pp. 5th Robin Miller
mystery.   ISBN 1-56280-156-2   10.95

CLASS REUNION by Linda Hill. 176 pp. The girl from her past . . .
                                                 ISBN 1-56280-178-3   11.95